Grimmtastic Girls
Gretel Pushes Back

Grimmtastic Girls

Cinderella Stays Late

Red Riding Hood Gets Lost

Snow White Lucks Out

Rapunzel Cuts Loose

Sleeping Beauty Dreams Big

Goldilocks Breaks In

Snowflake Freezes Up

Gretel Pushes Back

Grimmtastic Girls

Gretel Pushes Back

Joan Holub & Suzanne Williams

Scholastic Inc.

Text copyright © 2016 by Joan Holub and Suzanne Williams

All rights reserved. Published by Scholastic Inc., *Publishers since 1920.* SCHOLASTIC and associated logos are trademarks and/or registered trademarks of Scholastic Inc.

The publisher does not have any control over and does not assume any responsibility for author or third-party websites or their content.

ISBN 978-0-545-94535-6

10 9 8 7 6 5 4 3 2   16 17 18 19 20

Printed in the U.S.A.   40
First printing 2016

Book design by Yaffa Jaskoll

For our grimmawesome Grimmtastic Girls readers:

Jolee S., Jenna S., Sarah S., Tristyn R., Julia K., Kristen S.,
Annabelle Rose M., Shadia D., Cheyanne W., Lilly G.,
Julie K., Jasmine R., Charlie G., Patrona C., Sarah A.,
Aubrey B., Hannah L., Addy S., Harley R., Bryanna G.,
Rachael W., Kaydence D., Kathryn C., Becca R., Cindy B.,
Amanda B., Maddy W. and Aijay W., Jayla M., Danielle T.,
Christine D-H., Khanya S., Caitlin and Hannah R., Rachel B.,
Reegan C., Sloane C., Kyria T., Nolonna D., and you!

— JH and SW

Contents

1   Rain, Rain, Go Away   1

2   Hansel   10

3   An Errand   19

4   Eye of Newt Stew   37

5   Pathfinding   50

6   Into the Woods   61

7   Thump!   75

8   Hansel   83

9   Sticking It Out   89

10   A Proper Meal   97

11   Hansel   106

12   Hansel   118

13   Sister Act   124

14   Good Twin, Evil Twin   136

15   The Great Bake-Off   146

16   Help!   154

17   Happy Trails   170

It is written upon the wall of the Great Grimmstone Library:

Something E.V.I.L. this way comes.
To protect all that is born of fairy-tale, folktale, and nursery-
rhyme magic, we have created the realm of Grimmlandia. In
the center of this realm, we have built two castles on opposite
ends of a Great Hall, which straddles the Once Upon River. And
this haven shall be forever known as the Grimm Academy.

~ The brothers Grimm

Rain, Rain, Go Away

Gretel sat atop her high canopy bed in her dorm room at Grimm Academy on Friday afternoon, thumbing through her favorite book, *A Guide to Trails and Hikes Around Grimmlandia*. School was out for the day and she'd hoped to go hiking in the forest. Because she had a goal. One she had been thinking of for a while and had finally decided to pursue. She planned to discover new trails on her own and write a supplement to her favorite guidebook!

However, it looked like that wasn't going to happen today because it was raining. *Again.*

Hearing a noise, she looked up to see her roommate, Red Riding Hood, come in through the pearl-studded white curtain that served as the door to their small room. Gretel snapped her dog-eared guidebook shut. "Mmm," she said, sniffing the air and eyeing the plate of freshly baked cookies Red held in her hands. "Those smell grimmyummy! What kind are they?"

"Oatmeal," Red said. "Want some?" There was a twinkle in her brown eyes as she asked. Everyone at the Academy knew that Gretel was a total cookie monster. She'd never yet met a cookie she didn't love.

"Ooh! Oatmeal is my favorite!" Gretel exclaimed. She scrambled down the ladder at the end of her bed and dropped the guidebook on her desk. The beds in the girls' dorms at GA were each built like the top of a bunk bed. That way they were high enough off the floor that there was room for a desk and storage space below.

"Ha!" Red's long, dark curly hair, which had glittery red streaks in it, fell forward as she held the plate out to Gretel. "Your *favorite* is whatever I happen to bake!"

Red's tower-task assignment (all students got them — usually at the beginning of the school year) was Snackmaker. Cookies were her specialty. She made sure the cookie jar in the common room of Pearl Tower was always full, though it could be a real challenge with Gretel around!

"True," Gretel admitted, wiggling her eyebrows up and down mischievously. She snatched a couple of cookies off the plate and bit into one of them. "Mmm. Definitely grimm-yummy!" she murmured.

"Watch the crumbs," Red reminded her as bits of the cookie broke off and fell onto the brightly colored rug between their beds.

"Oops. Sorry," Gretel mumbled. For some reason, she couldn't seem to eat anything without making a mess, which drove her roommate crazy at times. She flipped her thick brown braid over one shoulder, then stooped. After scooping up the fallen crumbs, she tossed them into the trash can beside her built-in desk.

"I'll have my basket fetch us some napkins," Red said quickly. She stepped over to her desk and set the plate of cookies on top. Then she picked up a cute nut-brown wicker basket that also sat there. A bit bigger than a shoe box, the basket had a swirly design on either end, double handles, and a lid that hinged in the middle.

The basket was Red's magic charm. One day after Drama class, it had chosen her — by chasing after her on its own! To be chosen by a charm was quite an honor. Some students waited *years* to get charms. Although several of Gretel's friends had gotten theirs already, she was still waiting for hers.

Magic charms all had different powers. Usually it was up to the person they chose to discover just what their charm could do. Red's basket, for example, could fetch things that were small enough to fit inside it if asked in just the right way. And only if *Red* did the asking.

"A tisket, a tasket," Red said to her basket now. "Please fetch two big napkins, basket." The request part of her command always had to be phrased in six words. No more and no less.

A few seconds later, Red lifted her basket's lid and pulled out two large red-and-white-checkered cloth napkins. She handed one to Gretel.

After setting her basket down again, Red grabbed a cookie, too. She neatly tucked it halfway into her napkin and stepped over to the window on the far wall, between their beds. Nibbling at her cookie, she looked outside. "Still raining, I see," she commented.

"Mm-hmm," Gretel replied glumly as she ate. "This makes three rainy days in a row so far. I'm pretty sure Grimm Academy is going to be sitting in a swamp soon. I really wish it would stop pouring so I could go out hiking," she said wistfully.

She went to stand next to Red at the window. From there they could see that, because of all the rain, the Once Upon River was in danger of flooding its banks!

Red sighed. "I hear you. Staying indoors day in and day out makes me feel grimmgrumpy. Cinderella and I borrowed school umbrellas and tried going for a walk yesterday, but the wind was so fierce our umbrellas blew inside out before we could even get across the Pink Castle drawbridge."

Their dorm room was on the sixth floor and Gretel could see from the swaying trees below that the winds were still gusting. *Sigh.* Would this rain ever end?

Pearl Tower was one of three dorm towers that topped Pink Castle. The other two were Emerald Tower and Ruby Tower. All the girls who attended the Academy had most of their classes in Pink Castle. And except for a few girls like Rapunzel and Mermily, most of them slept in the dorms up top, too. The boys stayed mostly in Gray Castle on the opposite side of the river. Their dorm towers were named Onyx, Topaz, and Zircon.

Gretel finished her first cookie and began eating her second, being careful to catch crumbs in her napkin this time. A few still escaped somehow, though, and when Red wasn't looking, she scooted them under the rug between their beds.

Still munching, she went over to her desk and randomly opened her Grimmlandia hiking guidebook again. It fell open to a map and description of a trail called Mossy Cartwheels. She'd been on that trail and knew that its name came from the magical silvery moss that tumbled head over heels along it.

There were actually very few trails in this book that she hadn't already hiked multiple times. The only ones she avoided were those that ran through Neverwood Forest. Because, as a boy in her Grimm History class named Prince Awesome had once said, anyone with half a brain *never would* go there.

"I'm *soo* ready to hike," she told Red. "I think I'd even tramp through Neverwood Forest or into the Dark Nothingterror, just to get out of here for a while."

Red turned from the window and grinned at her. "Well, don't let Mr. Hump-Dumpty hear you say that. Or you'll get a lecture for sure." Their Grimm History teacher was always warning students of the dangers of Neverwood Forest and the Dark Nothingterror beyond it, which was filled with Barbarians and Dastardlies. He imagined that danger lurked pretty much everywhere, so he warned them about practically any other place they might want to wander as well.

Gretel sighed again and flung herself into the chair at her desk. "I've got cabin fever . . . er . . . make that *castle* fever, and it's only going to get worse each day this *grimmyucky* weather keeps us inside!"

"Why don't you come help me bake?" Red suggested, cocking her head at Gretel. "I've got another batch of cookies in the dorm oven I need to check on."

"No, that's okay. Baking's not my thing, as you know." She grinned. "Eating the results is, though!" She eyed the remaining cookies on the plate and licked her lips.

"Okay, I can take a hint," Red told her, grinning back. "I'll leave the rest of them here for you, but don't go crazy. Dinner's just a couple of hours away." She set the plate on her desk, then headed for their curtain door. "See you later, Cookie-nator."

"Later," Gretel echoed. Then Red was gone.

Feeling like a lion in a cage probably feels, Gretel began to pace up and down the small room. Twelve steps to the door and twelve steps returning to the window, back and forth. Along the way, she recited a nursery rhyme from one of the books in the Grimmstone Library to the beat of her footsteps. "Rain, rain, go away. Come again another day. Little Johnny wants to play." Frowning, she muttered to herself, "Make that little *Gretel* wants to play, or hike, anyway!"

Speaking of nursery rhymes, she wondered what her best friends, twins named Jack and Jill, were up to. Gretel and her brother Hansel often went hiking with the twins, whose favorite hikes were the hilly ones, going up one hill and down again.

She hadn't seen Jack or Jill since lunch. Just when she was thinking she'd go find them and see if they wanted to play a board game or something, she heard a familiar voice at the door. "Knock, knock." Gretel stopped pacing as Jill poked her curly blond head around the pearly curtain.

"Perfect timing!" Gretel exclaimed to her friend, happily waving her inside. "I was just thinking about you and wondering if you and Jack might want to hang out. Maybe play a game of Grimmopoly or that game Grimm of Thrones, since the rain's still coming down?"

Jill ventured a few more steps into the room. "Actually, I was just coming to tell you that Jack took a spill going downstairs after fourth period today. He's in the infirmary."

"Oh, no!" said Gretel. Jack was the klutziest person she knew and was always falling down or getting scrapes or bruises somehow or another. The infirmary was practically his second home. Still, she felt bad for him each time he wound up there. Truth was, she'd had a secret crush on that boy for some time now. It was a double-triple-super secret, though. Not even Jill knew!

"Yeah," Jill went on. "The Doctor, the Nurse, and the Lady with the Alligator Purse all had to be called in to figure out if he needed stitches for a cut on his forehead."

"Poor Jack," Gretel said. But then she perked up. "Let's go visit him! He could still play a board game with us. Might make him feel better."

Jill shook her head. "I can't right now. I've got to go get my pail from the library. I'm conducting a fire drill in Emerald Tower."

Jack and Jill had a magic pail that was kept in the Academy's library whenever they weren't using it. The pail could expand till it was as large as a small boat and scoop up enormous amounts of water to dump on fires.

"You should go, though," Jill added quickly. "I'm sure hanging out with you would really cheer him up."

Was Jill hinting that her brother liked Gretel, too? Gretel found herself blushing. But then Jill pointed at the plate of cookies on top of Red's desk and added, "Especially if you brought him a few of those cookies."

"Oh, sure. Good idea," Gretel told her friend. She stepped over to Red's desk and picked up the plate. There were still about a half dozen cookies on it. "They're oatmeal. Want one?" she asked, holding out the plate to Jill.

Jill took one and crunched into it. "Mm. Phanks. Thah's goo. See woo," she said with her mouth full. Then she whisked back out through the curtain.

Cheered at the thought of seeing Jack soon, Gretel shook the crumbs from her napkin into her trash can. Then she wrapped the remaining cookies in the cloth napkin, tying its four corners together so the cookies couldn't fall out. After pulling her GA Handbook from her schoolbag to make space, she dropped the napkin of cookies inside and slung the bag's straps over one shoulder. Then she was off to visit Jack.

2

Hansel

As soon as classes were out on Friday, Hansel hurried downstairs to the Academy's infirmary in the basement of Gray Castle. He wanted to check on his friend Jack. The two of them had been on their way from Battle Science class on the third floor of the castle down to their fifth-period Grimm History of Barbarians and Dastardlies class on the first floor of Pink Castle earlier that day when Jack tripped and fell on the stairs. Hansel had been right beside him when it happened, but he hadn't been fast enough to grab Jack's arm and stop his fall.

Hansel felt really bad about that. After all, it had been *his* fault Jack tripped. Oh, he hadn't pushed him or anything, but he might as well have. It was a long way from the third floor of Gray Castle to the first floor of Pink Castle on the girls' side of the Academy, and Jack had been lagging behind. "If you don't hurry up, we're going to be late to class!" Hansel had grumbled over his shoulder as they started downstairs.

Jack had put on a burst of speed then. And seconds later, just as he caught up to Hansel, he'd tripped, lost his balance, and tumbled the rest of the way down the stairs. Thing was, Hansel knew Jack was clumsy and accident-prone, so he never should have urged him to hurry. Who cared if they'd been a couple of minutes late to class? The teacher, Mr. Hump-Dumpty, was a good egg. (*Literally.* The teacher was an enormous egg with arms and legs.) He would have understood.

"Hey!" Jack greeted Hansel cheerfully as he entered the infirmary. "Did you come to break me out of here?" He was sitting on the edge of one of the infirmary's two beds with his legs hanging over the side as the Lady with the Alligator Purse handed him a glass of water and a couple of bright blue pills.

Hansel cringed at the sight of the lumpy bandage on Jack's forehead. "How many stitches did he get?" he asked the Lady with the Alligator Purse as Jack gulped down some water with the pills.

"None, actually," she answered. "He was lucky this time. The bandage was enough to do the trick."

"Oh, good," said Hansel. Though he still felt responsible for Jack's fall, it was a relief to know Jack's injury wasn't as bad as it might have been.

The lady patted Jack fondly on the shoulder as he

handed the glass back to her. "This is not exactly a prison," she told him with a smile. "But you can 'break out' of here now if you like."

"Grimmtasmagoric!" yelled Jack. He jumped down from the bed and grabbed his schoolbag from the floor. "See you later, Alligator . . . Purse Lady."

"Not too soon, I hope," she replied, her eyes twinkling at his little joke. "Once you leave here, I suggest you lie down in your room for a while and take it easy. And remember what I said earlier — you'll grow out of this clumsiness eventually when your feet catch up to your energy level. Until that happens, think before you step. Pay more attention to your surroundings."

"Yes, ma'am!" said Jack. Grinning, he gave her a mock salute. Unfortunately, as he saluted, he accidentally hit his elbow on the corner of the pill cabinet where she was working. *Bam!* "Ow!" he yelled, rubbing the injury with his opposite hand.

Smiling and shaking her head, the Alligator Purse Lady checked Jack's elbow. "Just a slight bruise."

She glanced at Hansel and added, "Keep an eye on our boy. Make sure he gets some rest. And try to keep him out of harm's way if you can."

"Will do," said Hansel. And he silently vowed to try harder to do just that. But it wouldn't be easy. The Lady was right about Jack. He was a ball of energy. Adventur-ous, too.

As they started upstairs from the basement, Jack said, "I have a feeling the rain is going to stop soon. If I'm right, how about going for a hike before dinner? I'm dying to get outside and get moving."

"Huh?" asked Hansel. "Have you already forgotten what the Alligator Purse Lady said about taking it easy? Maybe you should go to our room and take a nap instead." Besides being friends, the two of them were roommates.

Jack rolled his eyes. "You and that lady worry too much. I feel fine. What I really need is fresh air and exercise!"

"Well . . ." Hansel began slowly. It was tempting. He kind of felt like hiking himself. "Okay, *if* the rain stops, I guess we could go out for a while. If you promise to be care-ful. No running up and down muddy hills, or —"

"Yes, sir!" Jack interrupted, giving him a salute now, too. Then speaking casually, he added, "So if the rain does stop like you said, do you want to see if Gretel can come with us?"

"Sure. Hey, you aren't starting to get a crush on my sis-ter, I hope. I mean, you're always asking her along," Hansel teased. He was only joking, of course.

However, at the mention of crushing, Jack looked away, avoiding Hansel's eyes. Hansel frowned. Could things be

13

changing now that they were in middle school? Nah. He was just imagining stuff, he told himself. It made total sense that Jack would want to include Gretel on their hikes. They were all friends. In fact, Jack's twin sister, Jill, was Gretel's *best* friend.

Besides, in the same way Jack liked hiking with Gretel, Hansel liked hiking with Jill. Didn't mean Hansel was crushing on Jack's sister. He wasn't. They were all just pals, same as always.

Caught by surprise, Jack took a step backward. He bumped into Hansel and both boys almost went down. They had to scramble to regain their footing.

"Watch out, you klutzes! You almost knocked us down," complained Malorette. She and Odette stood on the first-floor landing.

Hansel could feel himself flush. Did the Steps have to always be so totally rude! What happened to that nursery rhyme he'd once read in the Grimmstone Library about girls being sugar and spice and everything nice? That rhyme did not apply in their case at all. They were more like snickers and spite and everything impolite.

Odette's dark eyes fastened on the bandage on Jack's forehead. She let out a cackle. "What happened to you?" she asked in a voice that was completely lacking concern or empathy.

"Let me guess," said Malorette. "You fell down again, right?" Her voice was so shrill that Hansel wished he could cover his ears. But he was more polite than these sisters, so he didn't.

Both girls laughed as if Jack getting hurt was the funniest thing ever. "You've got to be the clumsiest person in all of Grimmlandia!" Odette exclaimed.

Before Hansel could tell them off, however, Jack spoke up. "That's where you're wrong," he said good-naturedly. "I'm not just the clumsiest person in Grimmlandia, I'm the clumsiest person in all possible realms. Including the Dark Nothingterror." He smiled at them. "Not that I've ever been there. Just guessing."

"And," he went on, "I don't just trip over stairs and hills. Anyone can trip on uneven surfaces like those. However, it takes great skill like mine to trip on flat surfaces, especially when nothing's in your way. See? Watch this."

He took a step in their direction, then pretended to trip and tumble toward them. The girls shrieked, dropped their books, and stretched their hands out to ward him off. At the last second, before he could crash into them, he caught himself and straightened again.

The sisters glared at him, realizing he'd scared them on purpose. "You're crazy," Malorette announced, scowling.

Jack touched a fingertip to his bandage and nodded. "Too many injuries to the head can do that to a person," he agreed pleasantly.

Hansel had to hand it to Jack. He sure knew how to handle these sisters. Clearing his throat, he said, "Well, as much as we'd like to stay and chat, we've got stuff to do."

Both boys reached down to pick up the books the girls had dropped. All GA students had to take Comportment, an etiquette class taught by Ms. Queenharts. The boys had learned manners in that class even if these girls had not.

"Yeah," Jack agreed as he gave Malorette her books. "I don't hear the rain outside anymore. Think maybe it stopped?" he asked Hansel.

"I heard somebody say it was only drizzling now," Odette said, suddenly becoming interested enough in the conversation to briefly turn off the nastiness. "Why do you guys care?"

Hansel handed over her books with a shrug. "It's easier to hike when it's not raining."

The girls shared a quick, secretive look. "So you like to hike?" Malorette asked, blocking the boys' way now on purpose. "How good are you at following a trail map?"

Huh? That was a strange question, thought Hansel. But he answered it anyway. "Superb. That means *very* good, by the way. Gretel and I have been hiking trails almost from the time we were old enough to walk!" he couldn't help boasting.

Jack nodded. "It's the truth," he told the sisters. "They're the best."

"Good to know," said Malorette. She and Odette exchanged another sly look.

What was that about? Hansel wondered briefly. However, these two sisters were always exchanging sly looks, so he promptly let the question go. *Whatever!*

"Later, klutzes," Odette said. She and Malorette pushed past the boys and continued down toward the basement, their dark-haired heads close together as they whispered.

"Wonder where they're going," murmured Jack. "I have a feeling they're up to something."

"Yeah, what else is new?" Hansel replied as they continued up the Gray Castle stairs. "Maybe they're going to the infirmary to have their heads examined."

Jack laughed. Then he began taking the stairs upward two at a time. "Let's get to our room and grab our boots. Even if it's drizzling, we still might be able to get out and hike for a while!"

"Okay, but slow down!" Hansel cautioned. "Or do you want to end up in the infirmary again?"

Jack laughed. "You're such a worrywart!" Then his feet tangled and he tripped.

Hansel leaped to try to prevent disaster, but before he got there, Jack sprang up and shot him a big grin. He'd only been pretending to fall, like he had with those sisters!

"Ha-ha! Just joking!" Jack called back to him. "C'mon, get a move on!"

3

An Errand

On her way to the infirmary to see Jack, Gretel first crossed the stone walkway that ran between the Pink Castle's three towers. At the sixth-floor landing, she took a twisty staircase down to the fourth floor, then continued down the majestic grand staircase to the first floor.

As she zipped through the corridor heading for the Great Hall, she couldn't resist running a hand over the castle's stone walls. They were cool to the touch, and a pale pink color that reminded her of frosted valentine cookies.

Here and there the walls were hung with tapestries showing scenes of feasts and pageantry. And every so often, Gretel would pass one of the tall stone support columns whose tops were carved with figures of fantastical flowers, birds, and gargoyles. The flowers and birds looked so real she could almost imagine she was actually out in Grimmlandia hiking!

Oh, grindlesnorts! Her footsteps began to slow and grow less eager as she approached the Great Hall. The infirmary was in the basement of Gray Castle, on the opposite bank of the Once Upon River from Pink Castle. Since the Great Hall spanned the river, stretching over it like a tall bridge between the two castles, students could cross through the Hall to get to either castle.

However, if she'd remembered in time, she'd have crossed over on the fourth floor instead. She'd been thinking she could go outside and use one of the swan-shaped boats docked along the river to take the alternate water route to Gray Castle. She'd forgotten that the rain would mean the boat idea was out for today. Still, she didn't want to go all the way back up to the fourth floor, so . . . that left one choice. Crossing through the Great Hall.

She paused at its entrance, more than a little reluctant. Although the two-story Hall was a magnificent sight, there was something — or rather, someone — inside it that she hoped to avoid.

As quietly as possible she opened the door and began to tiptoe. Concentrating on trying not to even breathe very loudly, she hardly noticed the colorful banners on the walls, the high balconies at either end, or the two linen-draped tables that ran the entire length of the Hall, one along each wall. This was where dancing classes and balls were held, but mainly it was where meals were served. And it was the person who cooked those meals that she was trying to avoid.

Light streamed into the long room through rows and rows of windows with beautiful diamond-shaped glass panes as Gretel tiptoed on. As usual, some of the windows were propped open. Birds were flying in and out of the Hall, crossing in on one side and zooming back out the other. Many of them were super-helpful bluebirds. They could be summoned to deliver messages, and they also picked up empty trays after every meal and returned them to the kitchen.

Bang! Clank!

Uh-oh. Dinner wasn't for another couple of hours yet, but it sounded like the Head Cook, Mistress Hagscorch, was already setting up in the serving area. As she banged around bins filled with salad ingredients and whatever else was on today's menu, Gretel tried to sneak past.

Not that long ago, Gretel had refused to eat her meals in the Great Hall because of terrifying nightmares about this very cook. In the nightmares, Gretel would be putting loaves of bread into an oven to bake, when Mistress Hagscorch would suddenly sneak up behind her. Then the cook would give Gretel a push and send her tumbling into the red-hot oven! It was at that point that she always woke up screaming. Which had understandably kind of annoyed her roomie, Red.

Good thing she'd sort of, mostly, gotten over her fear of the cook by now. She was trying to become braver about other things as well, slowly but surely. Still, even though she hadn't had a nightmare about the witchy cook in a long while, she never went out of her way to talk to her. But this time, before Gretel could tiptoe past her, Mistress Hagscorch glanced up and saw her.

Gretel froze in her tracks, a sickly grin on her face. "Uh, hi, Mistress Scary — um, Mistress *Hag*scorch." *Oops!* She'd almost slipped and called the cook by one of the many nicknames she'd made up for her, such as Mistress *Scary*scorch or Mistress Frightwig. Names she was never so impolite as to actually call the cook out loud!

With eyes as yellow as a cat's and wild, scraggly white-gray hair, Mistress Hagscorch did look like a witch. And Gretel had always feared witches. Because, well, who didn't?!

Grinning at her now, Cook Witchyface licked her lips as if imagining some new recipe for a dessert — like Gretel pie, perhaps. Then she beckoned to Gretel with the crooked fingers of one clawed hand.

"Come here a moment, dearie. You look like a tasty treat" — Gretel let out a gasp at this, causing the cook to startle momentarily, but then the cook finished what she'd been about to say — "wouldn't do you a bit of harm."

With that, Mistress Bloodcurdler held out a green-colored cookie cut in the shape of a fat foot. "I call them troll toes." She pointed to the five slivered almond "toes" sticking out from one end of the cookie foot. "It's a new recipe and I need a student opinion."

Unable to come up with a reason not to try it (and being a huge cookie monster besides), Gretel sidled over and took the treat. Quickly, she took a step back. Then she bit into the foot cookie, and chewed it thoughtfully.

"So? What do you think?" the cook asked, sounding a bit anxious. "Are they sweet enough? And how's the texture? Not too chewy, I hope?"

Gretel swallowed and gave Hagscorch a thumbs-up. "Delish," she pronounced. "Not too sweet and not too chewy, but just right." It was the kind of thing a girl at school named Goldilocks would probably have said to describe the cookie. "*Toe*-tally awesome," she added.

The cook cackled at Gretel's pun. Then she reached way over the serving counter to pinch her cheek. "I like you, girl. You're so sweet I could eat you up!"

Though she knew Hagscorch was simply repeating a figure of speech, a shiver ran down Gretel's spine. She took a few more steps back. "Uh . . . thanks," she mumbled, looking toward the exit. "Well ... um ... it's been toe-tastic, but I've gotta go."

Gretel shoved the rest of the cookie into her mouth. Smiling around her mouthful of crunchy goodness, she waved good-bye.

Once she reached the western end of the Great Hall, she breathed a big sigh of relief. *Made it!* Pushing through the door, she started down some steps to the basement of Gray Castle. When she entered the infirmary, however, she found that its two beds were both tidily made and empty. Her shoulders drooped with disappointment. She'd been so jazzed about seeing Jack! Where was he?

Just then, in came the Doctor, in came the Nurse, and in came the Lady with the Alligator Purse. The Doctor and Nurse immediately decided Gretel must be ill and zoomed over to diagnose her.

"Mumps!" said the Doctor.

"Measles!" countered the Nurse.

"Wait! I don't think Gretel's here because she's sick! Am I right, Gretel?" asked the Alligator Purse Lady. Since Gretel had visited Jack for various injuries many times over the last few years, she was well known to the infirmary staff by this point.

"I was just looking for Jack," Gretel told her.

"Thought so," said the lady. "He's probably back in his dorm room by now."

"So you aren't sick?" the Doctor asked, sounding disappointed.

Gretel shook her head. "No, sorry."

He and the Nurse sighed. Then out went the Doctor and out went the Nurse.

However, the Lady with the Alligator Purse stayed behind. She took some bottles of pills and tubes of ointment out of her large purse and began organizing them in a nearby cupboard. "Jack didn't need stitches today. Just a bandage. Good thing that boy heals fast."

"That *is* lucky," said Gretel. Still, she'd really been hoping for a chance to hang out with him today. She stood in the middle of the room for a moment, feeling disappointed and swinging her schoolbag back and forth as she wondered what she should do next. Girls weren't allowed in the boys' dorms and vice versa. She could send Jack a message though. However, just as she was thinking about finding a paper and pen to write one and then calling on a bluebird to deliver it to him, the Lady with the Alligator Purse glanced at her over one shoulder.

"Would you mind running an errand for me?" she asked Gretel.

"Sure! I'd be happy to," Gretel replied, brightening. Whatever it was, it would be something to do, anyway. And she genuinely liked helping others. Which was probably why she'd been assigned the tower task of Pathfinder at the beginning of the year. The task involved helping other girls in her dorm find a path to friendship whenever they were having trouble getting along. "What would you like me to do?" she asked.

"Do you know where the candlestick-maker works?" asked the Lady as she fluffed up the bed pillows. When Gretel shook her head no, the Lady pointed down at the floor. "In a ship-shaped room below us in the dungeon. Could you go tell him I need two dozen candles?"

"Yeah. No problem," said Gretel. Excitement bubbled up in her. Although she'd been almost everywhere students were allowed to go in both castles, this was someplace new to explore. She hadn't even realized Gray Castle *had* a dungeon! Though why wouldn't it, since Pink Castle had one? she thought as she left the infirmary. In fact, Rapunzel, a girl who looked kind of goth, had actually gotten permission to sleep in a room in Pink Castle's dungeon with her five pet cats.

It took only a few minutes of searching around the basement to find a door to stairs leading down. When Gretel reached the bottom of these, she went along a wall until she saw what looked like the side of an actual full-size ship.

"How did you get here?" she wondered aloud. Had this ship been wrecked on the shores of the Once Upon River a long time ago? Maybe it had, and had proven so difficult to move that it eventually got built into the castle's dungeon!

Pausing before a small door cut into the ship's hull, she studied the big round lifesaver ring hanging on it. Painted in red upon the white ring were the words THE TUB.

She raised her fist to the door. *Knock. Knock. Knock.* Although she could hear voices inside, no one answered her knocking. She put her ear to the door and listened for a bit. She heard words like "That porthole . . . job . . . built . . . not my problem . . ."

None of that made any sense to her, probably because she couldn't hear the conversation very clearly. The voices were talking over one another and were a little muffled besides. She knocked louder. When still no one came, she let herself in.

Instantly, all talking in The Tub stopped and five sets of eyes turned to stare at her.

"What are you doing here?" grumped a girl she immediately recognized as Malorette. Apparently, Gretel had interrupted a private conversation that she and her sister,

Odette, were having with three stout men, who were each no taller than the girls themselves.

The two black-haired sisters were Cinderella's Steps (as in stepsisters) and were also major bad news. Gretel didn't really know them all that well herself, but she'd heard a lot about them because Cinderella was one of Red Riding Hood's BFFs, along with Snow White and Rapunzel. And it had been pretty obvious that Cinderella had had difficulties with her stepsisters from her very first day at the Academy.

"I came to get candles for the infirmary," Gretel announced, looking around the neat, shipshape room. "The Lady with the Alligator Purse sent me."

"Well, that's illuminating," said one of the three small men. He wore an apron that had scorch marks on it here and there.

"Wait! We weren't finished. What about the —" Odette started to say to him.

"I think we've about covered that whole ball of wax," the man in the scorched apron interrupted.

"Right! So why don't we cut this visit of yours short?" a second man said to the stepsisters. He was sharpening an assortment of big knives.

Scorched Apron Guy turned toward Gretel again, saying, "I'll help you. I'm the candlestick-maker."

Aha! That explained the scorches. They were probably from accidental candle flame burns.

Stepping briskly away from the others, he went over to a pot at the back of the room. Above the pot dangled many wax-coated wicks attached to a paddle. Newly made candles! Quickly, he took some of them down for her.

The other two men got back to work, too. After moving to a freestanding countertop at the front of The Tub (or maybe the *bow* since this was a ship?), the one with the knives put on a butcher's apron and began to slice a slab of meat. And the one who wore a tall white chef's hat — a baker? — started punching down some dough rising in a bowl.

In the meantime, Malorette and Odette slunk over to Gretel. Curling her lips as if she'd just bitten into a very sour lemon, Odette spoke to her in a harsh whisper. "What are you up to? Come here to spy?"

"Yeah, I bet she *is* a spy," Malorette echoed shrilly. To Gretel, she said, "You'll keep your nose out of things that don't concern you if you know what's good for you."

Gretel looked at the two sisters in surprise. "My nose isn't into anything," she sputtered. She'd meant to say she wasn't up to anything, but they probably got the idea.

Overhearing, the baker shook his head. "Never mind those two," he told Gretel. "They're as nutty as fruitcakes."

The butcher nodded in agreement. "Any way you slice it, you two are out of line," he admonished the sisters, waving his knife in the air.

Gretel took a few steps away from the sour sisters, who were continuing to give her the evil eye. If they suspected her of spying on them, that could mean only one thing. That they were up to something that was worth spying on. But what?

It was common knowledge at Grimm Academy that the sisters were members of a group called the E.V.I.L. Society, or they had been till the Society disbanded recently. The letters stood for Exceptional Villains in Literature, which was how the members liked to think of themselves.

"Heard anything from Ms. Wicked lately?" Gretel asked the girls, mostly to see what they'd say back.

Ms. Wicked, a teacher at GA and close associate of the sisters, had been a leader of the Society. For some reason it had always been plotting to take over GA and break down the barriers between Grimmlandia and the Nothingterror. But when E.V.I.L.'s efforts were thwarted, Ms. Wicked had escaped to an unknown location through one of her many magic mirrors. Upon her disappearance, everyone at the Academy had begun to hope the Society had become totally extinct.

Or *had* it? *Hmm.* Gretel smelled a mystery. Or maybe

that was just one of the pies the baker was baking? Either way, something smelled interesting.

"That's none of your beeswax," huffed Malorette, flipping her hair.

"Yeah," agreed Odette, copying the hair flip.

As the candlestick-maker came up to the counter and handed Gretel the candles he'd cut down and bundled together for her, Malorette glared in turn at him, the butcher, and the baker. "Anyway, all we came down here to say is that you can't tell us you didn't know what you were getting into," she told the men in her high-pitched voice.

"Okay, you've told us. So why don't you two take your noses and your beeswax out of here now that our business is done," said the candlestick-maker.

"*Humph!* Don't mind if we do," Odette sniffed scornfully. "Just remember you were well paid for your work. And for your silence!" With that, the two girls turned on their slippered heels and flounced out the door.

Gretel watched them leave and then asked the men lightly, "What was that about?"

"A stew over nothing," the butcher assured her as he and the other two men traded meaningful glances.

"Those two just enjoy fanning the flames of conflict," said the candlestick-maker.

"And stirring up trouble," added the baker.

Gretel stood there for a moment, looking from one stout man to another and feeling puzzled. Something was definitely going on, but it seemed plain these guys weren't going to tell her what it was! They must've wanted to discuss things privately among themselves, though, because all of a sudden they ushered her to the door.

"Sorry you have to *cut* out so soon," said the butcher, holding it open for her.

"But you really don't want to be *loaf*ing around here," said the baker.

"Do tell the Lady with the Alligator Purse we hope those candles will *light* up her life . . . or at least the infirmary!" the candlestick-maker said. Then he gave Gretel a little push out into the hall.

Bam! The ship's door shut behind her.

"Well, that was interesting!" Gretel murmured, a little stunned at how fast they'd kicked her out.

Returning to the infirmary, she dropped the candles off and gave the Lady with the Alligator Purse the candlestick-maker's good wishes. Then she started back to her room again, crossing over the river on the fourth floor this time instead of making her way through the Great Hall.

After passing by offices and the auditorium on four, she took the twisty stairs back up to the sixth floor. When she entered the outdoor stone walkway again, she noticed something grimmawesome. The rain had finally stopped. *Hooray!*

There was still some daylight left. She could grab her hiking boots and head off down a trail. Not just any trail, either. It was time to try a new one. At last, she could finally get started on writing that supplement to her favorite guidebook! In a hurry now, she dashed to her dorm room.

Gretel was pulling on her boots when a bluebird pecked at her bedroom window. Noticing it had a note in its beak, she opened the window to let it in. The bird dropped the note in her hand and then flitted off. "Thank you," she called after it. It dipped a wing as if to say, *You're welcome!*

The note was from Hansel. It read, *Meet 4:15 in the Bouquet Garden if you want to go for a short hike.*

Hmm. Though she couldn't have said exactly why, she hadn't yet discussed with her brother her plan to map more trails and write a guidebook supplement. Maybe because she was afraid he'd tell her it was a dumb idea. Or that he might try to take over the project himself.

Oh, he wouldn't *mean* to take it over, but he'd have his own ideas about the "right way" to go about doing things. And somehow pretty soon the project would become more his than hers. That kind of thing had happened before with other projects she'd been part of. She definitely did not want it to happen this time.

Well, she supposed she could coax him into trying a new trail without telling him about her big idea to add to the guidebook, right? If he wasn't up for it, she'd put off her plans for new explorations till tomorrow. Because hiking with her brother was always more fun than going alone. In spite of his bossiness, he was her favorite hiking partner. Plus, maybe he would have some news to share about Jack!

Speaking of sharing, she decided she'd share Red's cookies with Hansel since Jack wasn't around. She grabbed her schoolbag again and clomped downstairs as fast as she could. Just then, the Hickory Dickory Dock clock over in the Great Hall bonged four thirty. The sound was piped throughout the Academy to keep everything going like clockwork.

"Oh, crumb cakes," thought Gretel, walking faster.

Once outside, she dashed around the side of Pink Castle to the Bouquet Garden, where the bushes actually bloomed with many kinds of flowers bunched together in ready-made bouquets. She arrived too late, though. Hansel wasn't there. Crouching among the bushes, she looked for signs of his boot prints in the wet grass. Because if she could figure out which way he'd gone hiking, maybe she could still catch up to him on the trail.

While she was crouched over, she suddenly heard foot-steps on the Pink Castle drawbridge. Soon the familiar voices of the two sour sisters reached her. They were coming her way. Her ears perked up when she heard Odette say, "So do you really think Gretel was spying on us?"

Jumpin' gingersnaps! she thought. If those two caught sight of her hiding like this, it would only seem to confirm their suspicions about spying. Even if her happening to be here now *was* just a coincidence. Quickly, she dove behind a thick hedge at the back of the garden as the sisters rounded the corner and drew closer.

"Not sure," Malorette said to Odette after a pause. "But we'd better go tell You-Know-Who that we suspect her, just in case."

Huh? Who was You-Know-Who? Gretel wondered. She really wished Malorette had been more specific!

"Yeah," Odette agreed. "You-Know-Who will want to know. And now that the butcher, the baker, and the candlestick-maker have finished building the portal, it won't be long till —" She hushed suddenly when shouts came from other students hanging out somewhere outside beyond the garden.

Portal? Had Gretel heard right? Outside the door of The Tub, she'd thought she'd heard a port*hole* mentioned. Were they the same thing? Or which one did the girls mean? And it wouldn't be long till *what* happened? She wondered.

She held her breath as the two sisters passed out of the garden. Too bad those shouts in the distance had interrupted Odette. Gretel would've liked to hear the rest of what she'd been intending to say! Peeking through the hedge, she watched the two girls disappear in the direction of Neverwood Forest.

Then a horrible thought struck her. What if the You-Know-Who they'd referred to was Ms. Wicked? Or Ludwig, the evil brother of Jacob and Wilhelm Grimm? What if they weren't in the Dark Nothingterror after all, as some people suspected? Maybe one or both of them was hiding out in the forest instead! Could the E.V.I.L. Society be starting up *again*? Or had it never really stopped existing? She needed to find out!

4

Eye of Newt Stew

Gretel started out of the garden, intending to follow Malorette and Odette into the forest and eavesdrop some more. But then she stopped, fearing they'd catch her at it. Besides, the thought of going into Neverwood Forest gave her the creeps. As did the thought of possibly coming face-to-face with Ms. Wicked or Ludwig Grimm — if that was who the stepsisters were actually planning to meet.

Was she being a coward? she asked herself. Or just using commonsense caution? Sometimes it was hard to know the difference. At the very least, she decided, she should share this information with the Grimm Organization of Defense.

Formed not long ago, G.O.O.D. was a student organization that aimed to defend Grimmlandia from all kinds of threats, whether they came from E.V.I.L., the Dark Nothingterror, or wherever!

Gretel did a quick about-face and was heading back to

the Pink Castle drawbridge when she heard a shout from behind her.

"Hey!"

She whirled back around. "Hansel!" she called out. She waved happily to him.

And he was with Jack! Her heart skipped a beat as the boys came toward her. The lumpy bandage on her secret crush's forehead didn't make him look any less cute, in her opinion. Just like his twin sister, Jill, he had curly blond hair. But unlike Jill, he had deep dimples in his cheeks that Gretel found adorable.

"Where were you?" Hansel asked once he and Jack had caught up to her. "We waited in the garden at least ten minutes, but you never showed."

Jack grinned. He seemed to be feeling fine, despite the newest bump on his head. "Hansel was worried about you, so I told him we should come back," he told her.

Frowning, Hansel ran a hand through his short-cropped brown hair, which had almost as many natural red highlights in it as Gretel's. "Was not. I was just getting hungry, that's all."

Gretel didn't believe him. Despite being only one year older than she was, her brother had always been very protective of her. She hadn't minded his protectiveness until recently. But more and more, she found it kind of annoying.

Especially since his protectiveness often resulted in *bossi-ness*. She was twelve years old now! Plenty old enough to take care of herself. And old enough to have her own ideas for how to do things, too.

Trying to keep the irritation out of her voice, she said to Hansel, "I didn't get your message till too late." Then she shifted her gaze to Jack. "Sorry about your accident. I went to the infirmary to see you, but you'd already left. Then I wound up running an errand for the Lady with the Alligator Purse." Her eyes flicked back to Hansel. "That's why I got your message late."

"What kind of errand?" Jack asked curiously as the three of them clomped in their hiking boots across the draw-bridge and back into Pink Castle.

"Well . . ." While they made their way toward the Great Hall for dinner, Gretel told the two boys about her trip to the Gray Castle dungeon to get candles from the candlestick-maker. "I didn't even know The Tub existed," she told them. Then she frowned. "Malorette and Odette were there when I went in."

Before she could go on, Jack made a face. "Let me guess. Did they say something nasty to you or try to trip you or something? Those girls are more hazardous than tree roots on a hiking trail or . . ." He began to name various hazards — all things he'd actually tripped over in the past.

When he took a breath in the middle of that long list, Gretel shook her head. "Not really, but they seemed to think I'd come to spy on them." She was about to tell the boys exactly what the sisters had said to her inside The Tub, and what she'd overheard while hiding outside in the Bouquet Garden. However, Hansel went into bossy mode and interrupted her before she could do so.

"I wish you hadn't drawn those girls' attention," he said. "I don't like or trust those two. You should stay far away from them."

Though Gretel's impulse had been to do exactly that — she hadn't followed them into the forest, after all — she resented Hansel telling her what to do.

She decided to push back a bit. "Hey, I'm not a little kid!" she told him indignantly. "I know better than to trust them." She was debating whether or not she should tell him what else the sisters had said — if she should share her suspicions about who they were going to see and how the men in The Tub had apparently built an important porthole or portal. But then Hansel added, "And I don't trust those Rub-A-Dub-Dub guys, either."

"Rub-A-Dub-Dub guys?" Gretel repeated. She reached for the castle door, but Jack was there ahead of her and opened it. He smiled at her, waving her through. She smiled back, distracted from her irritation for a moment.

"He's talking about the old nursery rhyme they're from," Jack noted with a laugh, once they were all inside. "Well, one version of it anyway." He recited it aloud. "*Rub-a-dub-dub, three men in a tub. And who do you think they be? The butcher, the baker, the candlestick-maker. Turn them out, knaves all three.*"

"Knaves are male servants with a reputation for dishonesty and trickery," Hansel informed her in that same bossy tone.

Gretel bristled again. "I know that," she said, even though she hadn't. She just didn't like Hansel thinking he knew more than she did, even if that was often the case when it came to the meanings of words. And no wonder. He actually read dictionaries just for fun!

She decided then and there to put off telling him till later about her (almost) encounter with Malorette and Odette in the Bouquet Garden. She would tell her friends instead. They were all members of G.O.O.D. Working together, she felt certain they could come up with a plan for dealing with the sour sisters' revelations.

As soon as she and the boys entered the Great Hall, Rose and Snowflake called to her. They were two of the Academy's newest students and were waving her over to join them in the serving line. With a quick bye to Hansel and Jack, Gretel peeled away and went to join her friends.

In the serving line, she took a tray and got behind Snowflake. The pretty blue-eyed girl had a heart-shaped face framed by long black hair and bangs. When she stepped up to the counter and ordered a plate of the eye of newt stew — which tasted much better than it sounded — Mistress Hagscorch cackled. "You look like you need fattening up," she told Snowflake. "I'll give you an extra-large serving!"

Gretel couldn't help shuddering. Snowflake only laughed, however, and brushed her longish bangs out of her eyes. "Your stew is the best!" she said, flashing Mistress Hagscorch a sweet smile.

"Why, thanks, missy." The cook grinned big. Which only made her look scarier, in Gretel's opinion.

What Snowflake had said about the stew was true. There was no denying that Hagscorch was a grimmfabulous cook. Still, Gretel had long ago decided it was best not to think about the ingredients that might or might not go into her tasty dishes.

Stepping up to the counter now, she held out her tray. "I'll have the stew, too, please," she said. Instantly, Scaryscorch's wrinkled old claw of a hand shot out to drop a plate of the stew onto Gretel's tray. "And, um, a gingerbread cookie?" Gretel added. She couldn't resist those three-dimensional cookies. Shaped like gingerbread houses, they were just big enough to fit in the palm of one's hand and were beautifully decorated with candies and icing.

The cook cackled. Then her hand shot out again and she pinched Gretel's cheek. "You like my cookies, don't you, sugardrop?" She gave her a wink. "Would you like another Troll Toe, too?"

"Yes, please," Gretel squeaked. Withdrawing her hand, Mistress Cheeksqueezer then dropped the two cookies onto her lunch tray. "Thanks," Gretel managed to say before scurrying away. Maybe she *was* a coward. She hoped not.

She sat down next to Snowflake at one of the Hall's two long tables. Soon Rose (aka Sleeping Beauty) plopped down on the bench on Gretel's other side. Across the table from the three girls were Jill, Cinderella, and Red.

Even if she was a coward, Gretel was glad to be brave enough to eat in the Great Hall nowadays. It was always fun to be around so many friends — as long as Hagscorch stayed in the kitchen. "So where did you disappear to this afternoon?" Red asked Gretel as the girls tucked into their food. "By the time I finished baking, you'd gone." Then she added with a grin, "And that cookie plate I brought was empty, too."

Gretel felt herself blush. There probably weren't any students at the Academy who *weren't* aware of what a cookie monster she was, but for once she had not eaten them all by herself! It took her a moment to reply, however, because she'd just taken her first bite of the eye of newt stew. As always, the stew boiled and bubbled (at just the right temperature) inside her throat. It was a slightly ticklish but delightful feeling.

Even after she swallowed, a few tiny bubbles that looked like real eyeballs escaped her mouth when she finally began to speak. "Actually, I put the extra cookies in my schoolbag to take to Jack, only he wasn't in the infirmary when I got there," she told Red. She hefted her bag onto her lap and pulled out the napkin full of cookies.

"Too bad for my brother," Jill said with a grin. Since she was also eating the stew, a few eyeball bubbles escaped her mouth as she spoke, too. "Hand 'em over. I promise I'll share some with Jack later on. Or at least one of them." Jill was almost as big a cookie monster as Gretel!

Smiling fondly at her BFF, Gretel handed her the bundle of cookies and returned her schoolbag to the floor. After gobbling down a few more bites of the tasty stew, Gretel decided to tell the girls at her table about her visit to The Tub and what she had heard Odette and Malorette say there and in the Bouquet Garden later on.

"I saw your Steps down in the Gray Castle dungeon

a little while ago, Cinderella," she said when there was a pause in the conversation. "They sure were acting strange."

"That's because they *are* strange," Cinderella said matter-of-factly. Which made all the girls crack up.

In an attempt to add her own bit of humor, Gretel said, "They aren't just strange. They really put the evil in E.V.I.L. In fact, they —"

Suddenly, Red was overcome by a coughing fit. "Are you okay?" Gretel interrupted herself to ask in concern. Red nodded, but at the same time she flicked her eyes meaningfully to something — or someone — beyond Gretel.

Gretel glanced over her shoulder. *Uh-oh.* Malorette and Odette, back from their forest trek, were standing right behind her! They both gave her super-sour looks before moving off toward the serving line to get their dinner.

It was clear they'd overheard what Gretel said about them, which made her feel kind of sorry. For two reasons: (1) because she didn't like being mean to anyone, and (2) because now they knew she was talking to others about them and E.V.I.L. But thank goodness she hadn't yet begun her story about what the sisters had said and her suspicions about them. If those two got an inkling that she suspected them of plotting trouble, they'd be way more careful to cover their tracks.

45

Then G.O.O.D. would have no chance of finding out what they were up to. Though the group didn't have regularly scheduled meetings (they had, in fact, met only a few times after forming and not at all since Ms. Wicked's disappearance), Gretel knew members would want to become more active if they believed E.V.I.L. was plotting trouble.

Despite her dislike and distrust of Malorette and Odette, Gretel felt another pang of regret. Even if what she'd said about them was true, she really didn't like the idea that she might've hurt their feelings. Maybe she should apologize when she got the chance?

The conversation had moved on by now, but after a little while, Cinderella spoke to Gretel. "So, my evil stepsisters. Was there something else you wanted to say about them?"

Gretel nodded. But just as she was about to launch into the things she'd wanted to talk about earlier, Malorette and Odette approached with their dinner trays. Giving Gretel the stink eye, they plopped down on the bench only a few students over from her. Had they sat close by just to make sure she didn't report on them to her friends? If so, their ploy worked.

"Uh . . . maybe later," Gretel murmured to Cinderella. For the rest of the meal, she stayed quiet. Because every time she slid her eyes sideways to check, she caught one or the other of the sisters glaring at her.

As dinner was ending, the enormous hickory-wood grandfather clock on the balcony at the Pink Castle end of the Hall began to speak. (There was an actual face on the front of the clock, complete with eyes, a nose, and a mouth.)

"Hickory Dickory Dock,
The mouse ran up the clock.
The clock strikes six.
Friends can now mix.
Hickory Dickory Dock."

A mechanical mouse popped out of a little door above the clock's face as soon as the rhyme ended. It squeaked cutely six times in a row to signal the hour, then six low-toned *bongs* echoed the hour throughout the rest of the Academy.

The bluebirds that had been flying back and forth through the open windows overhead suddenly dipped down to the tables. Working together in small groups, they picked up finished trays with their beaks and carried them off to the serving area. As always, they returned seconds later to set little silver bowls of water and new white linen napkins on the table in front of each student.

Gretel dipped her fingers into her bowl and then wiped them on her clean napkin. Afterward, in thanks for their service, she gave the birds a few cookie crumbs she'd saved for them.

Now everyone began to leave the Great Hall, off to mix with their friends, as the clock had put it. Most of the girls went toward Pink Castle, while the boys headed for Gray Castle. The girls Gretel had been sitting with had started to chatter about a catapulting game they planned to play on the rooftop courtyard that evening.

"Yeah, Rapunzel's the one to beat. Our current distance champion. Her last catapult made it to the far side of Ice Island, remember?" Ice Island, a recent magical creation of Snowflake's, sat in the middle of the Once Upon River right across from the Academy.

Gretel had been hoping for an opportunity to tell her friends more about Malorette and Odette. But unfortunately, she was painfully aware that those two sisters were walking directly behind her. *Literally* painfully aware. They'd been deliberately stepping on the heels of her boots every few steps as they all exited the Hall. She hadn't meant to make them her enemies!

"I'll catch up to you all later," she finally told the other girls as they reached the foot of the grand staircase and started upward. Summoning her courage, she then turned to face the sour sisters. "Just wanted to say I'm sorry if

I hurt your feelings at dinner. I didn't mean to," she told them sweetly.

Identical looks of surprise at her pleasant attitude crossed the sisters' faces but were soon replaced by their customary sneers. "Whatever," said Odette.

Malorette leaned in. "I think the three of us need to have a little chat. Somewhere private. Follow us." With that, she started down the hallway, and Odette gestured for Gretel to walk with them.

Gretel gulped. "Um. Okay." Feeling uneasy, she nevertheless followed the sisters down the hall. What was this going to be about? Nothing good, probably.

5

Pathfinding

Malorette and Odette stopped outside the door to the classroom where Ms. Wicked had taught before her disappearance, er, escape. She'd taught Scrying, which was the art of using crystal balls and other reflective surfaces such as mirrors to predict the future.

After casting her sister a secretive look, Malorette said to Gretel, "We can talk in here." She reached out and tried to turn the knob.

To Gretel's relief, the door was locked. "Guess we'll have to talk somewhere else. Maybe just here in the hall? No one's around." She really didn't want to go into Ms. Wicked's old classroom — or any other private space — with these two.

However, Malorette only grinned. "Not a problem." She produced a key from the pocket of her dark-blue velvet gown and promptly unlocked the door.

As Gretel reluctantly followed the sisters inside the classroom, she wondered briefly if Malorette had stolen the key from the office. But it was also possible that Ms. Wicked had given it to her some time ago. After all, the three of them had always been as thick as thieves. Maybe the teacher had even given them the key *that very afternoon*, if that's who they'd met in the forest before dinner!

Gretel shivered at the thought and gazed around the room. "It's creepy in here," she murmured, which made the sisters smile.

No one had been hired to replace Ms. Wicked yet. Since her students had been transferred to other classes, the room had an unused feeling about it. It was dim and dusty, and cobwebs were beginning to form here and there high in the corners.

But in other ways the room was the same as always. The square student tables still stood in the exact same places they'd always been for Scrying. And crystal balls of various sizes still sat on shelves, while small square mirrors about the size of playing cards hung in rows from little silver nails on the far wall.

Ms. Wicked's desk remained in its usual spot at the front of the classroom, along with a glass-fronted cabinet full of her strange books. In short, the room's contents were exactly the same as before the teacher's disappearance. Except that all of her many large mirrors were missing, including the one she'd used to write assignments on in red lipstick.

"Too bad about the mirrors," Odette said with a sigh.

"Yeah, I miss them," said Malorette, gazing around.

Rumor had it that all these missing mirrors, and even more from Ms. Wicked's living quarters, had been moved to an ice castle on Snowflake's Ice Island. The mirrors were later destroyed when the castle collapsed.

"Good riddance, I say," Gretel mumbled.

"What?" asked Odette.

"Nothing," said Gretel, giving her a fake smile. With bravado, she added, "So you wanted to talk?"

Malorette patted her poofy black hairdo while motioning with her other hand toward one of the square tables. "Sit," she said to Gretel.

Feeling a little jittery, Gretel pulled out one of the chairs at the table and sat. Her eyes went to the door, which was closed now. Odette came to stand over her, as if to make sure she didn't try to bolt for the exit. What were they plotting?

As Odette stood guard, Malorette wandered over to one of the shelves and picked up a crystal ball about the size of a grapefruit. Tossing it casually from hand to hand as if it were some kind of plaything, instead of a powerful magical object, she came back to the table and sat down across from Gretel.

"Your tower task in Pearl Tower is Pathfinder, right?" she asked.

The way Malorette was holding the crystal ball, Gretel could actually see herself reflected in it. Her braid was a mess with strands pulling free. It really needed a good brushing and rebraiding, she decided. But for now, she just finger-combed the strands back.

"Uh-huh," she replied. At the same time, she wondered how Malorette knew what her tower task was. The two sisters roomed together in Ruby Tower, and Gretel had no idea what *their* tasks were. Probably Trouble Causers, or Mischief Makers. She grinned at the idea.

"What's so funny?" Odette demanded. When Gretel just shrugged, Odette took the ball from her sister and set it in the center of the table. Then she sat, too, on Gretel's other side.

"And so you like to hike around a lot, right?" Malorette continued to Gretel. When she spoke she leaned forward, bringing her mouth so close to the ball that it was almost like she was speaking into it. *Weird!*

After Gretel nodded, Odette added, "We've seen you out and about with your brother and those twins with the pail." She leaned closer to the ball when she spoke, too.

"Yeah. Jack and Jill," Gretel informed them, wondering why these sisters had dragged her into this room just to play Twenty Questions.

But then Malorette told her, "Our pathfinding skills are not that great. We're looking for someone who can follow a trail better than we can. And we're wondering if that someone might be you?"

"Huh?" Gretel looked from one sister to the other in confusion. Then she started to laugh. "Oh! Ha-ha-ha. I get it! You think my tower task as Pathfinder means I lead other girls in my dorm on hiking paths around Grimmlandia?"

Odette frowned and looked over at Malorette, nudging the crystal ball closer to Gretel. "Well, isn't that what you do?" she asked.

Gretel's eyes were momentarily drawn to the ball and she startled for a split second, thinking she'd glimpsed a face inside it. Not hers, though. A face that looked a lot like Mistress Hagscorch! But in a split second there was nothing but smooth glass again. This creeped-out room must be making her imagination work overtime, she decided.

"Nuh-uh," Gretel finally said in answer to Odette's question. "Sorry, my task as Pathfinder is to help girls who aren't getting along well find paths to friendship."

Malorette leaped from her chair. Going over to Odette, she thumped her sister hard on the shoulder. "You idiot!"

she screeched. "Why didn't you check what her Pathfinder duties were?"

"Ow!" yelled Odette, jumping up, too. "That hurt!" She grabbed a fistful of her sister's dark hair and started to pull. "Why would I check? She hikes! You knew that!"

Gretel stood up. "Whoa!" she said, leaning toward the sisters. "Looks like you might benefit from my Pathfinder skills after all. How about letting go of Malorette's hair, Odette? Then you can each take five steps apart and breathe deeply a few times."

"Ha!" snorted Odette. But she did release her sister's hair.

Malorette straightened up, pushing her tousled hair back into its usual poof again. "We don't need any of your relationship-fixing mumbo jumbo," she told Gretel with a sniff. "Just tell us one thing. Can you find your way down a trail or not?"

"Course I can," said Gretel.

"Okay. Good," said Odette. Cupping both of her hands around the crystal ball, she lifted it from the table and stepped closer to Gretel. "We've got a job for you, then."

Gretel arched an eyebrow. "What? You want me to take you hiking?"

Odette and Malorette grinned at each other. Apparently, all was fine between them again. "That's exactly what we want," said Malorette as Odette handed off the ball to her.

Odette looked into Gretel's eyes. "Only we have to know if we can trust you. Can we?"

Malorette held the ball up high. "Because the path we want to find is a secret one," she added.

Odette smiled at Gretel. "And it goes to a secret place so magically beautiful you'll hardly believe it!"

Malorette nodded excitedly. "A place where colorful birds sing in lush gardens, and —"

"— and waterfalls tumble down cliffs of gold!" Odette finished.

"Really?" Gretel's heart began to beat fast. Despite not being as brave as she'd like to be, she'd always craved exploration and adventure. Finding such a fab place as they were describing would be *grimmcredible*! She could list it and the trail leading to it in the supplement she was planning to write. It would give her no small satisfaction to outdo her bossy older brother with such a find. But the girls had said it was secret. *Hmm.*

Doubt tugged at her. She moved toward the teacher's desk, just to put some distance between her and the sisters. "If it's such a secret path and place, then how do *you* know about it?" she asked with her back to them.

When she turned around again, she jerked her head in surprise. Because the sisters had rushed over and were holding the crystal ball so close to her it was almost like they wanted her to take a bite out of it. She took a quick step back.

"We . . . uh . . . learned about it from Mr. Hump-Dumpty," Odette informed Gretel. "He drew us a map."

Malorette reached into her pocket and pulled out a hand-drawn sketch on a piece of vellum paper. She dropped it onto Ms. Wicked's desk and set the crystal ball beside it. "Take a look."

While Gretel studied the crudely drawn map, Odette nervously wandered to where the Scrying mirrors hung and gave them a little push to set them swaying. When they brushed up against one another, they made a tinkling sound like wind chimes.

Gretel looked up from the map. "What's NWF?" She pointed to letters inked inside a big circle through which a curving line of dashes ran. (She figured the dashes were meant to represent the path.)

"Neverwood Forest," Malorette translated.

Gretel gasped. "But Mr. Hump-Dumpty is always warning everybody to stay *away* from that forest. It's dangerous!" In fact, she'd often heard their Grimm History teacher call it *"a place no one ever visited and lived to tell about afterward."*

"Grimmhooey," Malorette said calmly. "Mr. Hump-Dumpty goes there all the time himself."

"He does?" Gretel said in surprise. She'd hardly ever seen the big egg-shaped teacher outside the school grounds, and she'd definitely never seen him near the forest. But since she rarely went near the forest herself, why would she?

After giving the little mirrors one last push to set them tinkling again, Odette crossed back to the teacher's desk. With a sideways glance at her sister, she said, "Can you blame him for wanting to keep such a beautiful place all to himself? If lots of students went tramping around in the forest, it wouldn't stay secret for long."

Malorette nodded in agreement. Then, sneering at Gretel, she said, "But maybe you're too *afraid* to go into the forest." She grinned over at her sister. "Maybe we should ask someone older and braver to help us." She wrinkled her forehead as if considering other possible candidates. Then she snapped her fingers. "I know! We'll ask Hansel! He's more mature than Gretel, and he's probably a better hiker, too."

Gretel felt her cheeks redden hotly. "I am *not* afraid," she fibbed. "And I'm just as good a hiker as Hansel."

Malorette folded her arms and stared hard at her. "Then prove it."

"Okay! When do you want to go?" Gretel blustered.

"Tomorrow morning at nine," Odette answered quickly.

"But you can't tell anyone where we're going," Malorette cautioned as she snatched back her map. "Mr. Hump-Dumpty made us promise we wouldn't tell anyone about his secret place. If he knew we'd told you, he'd get really ticked off."

"Okay," Gretel agreed, though she couldn't imagine Mr. Hump-Dumpty getting ticked off about anything. He was most definitely a worrywart, but she'd never seen him get angry.

At her agreement, the sisters seemed to decide their business was finished for now. Malorette went over and set the crystal ball back on the shelf she'd taken it from. Then she and Odette headed for the door. Gretel followed them out and Malorette locked the door behind them. "Tomorrow, then," she said curtly to Gretel. Without another word, she and Odette took off down the hall.

Gretel went the opposite way. While climbing the grand staircase, she mulled over what the sisters had told her.

Some of it she wasn't sure she believed. If Mr. Hump-Dumpty really did have a secret place, it seemed unlikely he'd tell those two girls about it. Unless they'd tricked him somehow? Or maybe they'd stolen the map from his desk without his knowledge? No, unfortunately, it seemed much more likely that the secret place simply didn't exist. It was a little too good to be true even if magical things did happen in Grimmlandia all the time.

She thought briefly of sending the sisters a bluebird note and telling them she'd changed her mind about going hiking with them. But something stopped her. What if the magical place really *did* exist? If she backed out, they might take Hansel there. Then he'd be all superior because he got to see the secret place instead of her. No, as long as it wasn't raining tomorrow, she would go.

As she started up the twisty stairs to join her real friends, Gretel could hear them laughing and shouting up on the rooftop courtyard as they catapulted things from it toward the river. She'd better put off telling the members of G.O.O.D. or anyone else anything for now, she decided. Like Hansel, they might try to talk her out of going with Malorette and Odette. If it turned out those two were indeed up to some kind of real mischief, she would report it *after* their hike.

One thing was clear though. Whatever happened tomorrow, she would need to be careful to keep her wits about her with those tricky sisters!

6

Into the Woods

When Gretel got up the next morning, Red was already gone. Her roomie had said something about a Saturday morning play rehearsal when the girls were all catapulting stuff off the roof last night. It seemed that Red would be starring as the female lead in *Haplessly Ever After*, an upcoming play in which a series of funny misfortunes befall a prince and princess. Red's crush, Wolfgang (a boy who could shape-shift into a wolf), would star as the prince. They were the most talented actors at GA!

Gretel stood before the mirror that hung on the outside of her armoire and brushed out her red-brown hair. She had always worn it in the same braid, which reached her waist. Washing and drying her long, thick hair took a lot of time, however. Maybe she was ready for a change. To a style that looked . . . older.

On the spur of the moment, she grabbed some scissors from her desk drawer and started cutting. *Snip! Snip!* By the time she was done, her hair was a more medium length. It was curlier now, too, and bouncier. It felt good.

After dressing, Gretel packed a small, bright-blue back-pack with necessary hiking supplies like first-aid stuff, candles, matches, her cloak (in case it got cold), a canteen of water, and so forth. She also tossed in her trusty pocket-knife, which she never went hiking without. Finally, she pulled on her boots and laced them up.

Before leaving to meet Malorette and Odette out on the sixth-floor stone walkway as planned, Gretel paused to straighten the row of carved wooden animals on her desktop. Each figure was about four inches high. She'd carved them herself with her handy-dandy pocketknife. Among them were a crow with outstretched wings, a bear with a fish clasped in its paws, and a rabbit with tall, straight ears. She'd bumped the squirrel with a long, bushy tail out of line the day before and now moved it back into place.

Her grandfather had been famous for his woodcarving skills and Gretel liked to think she'd inherited some talent for the craft from him. Even when she was little, she'd loved watching him carve and he'd taught her the skill. And while they worked at it together, he'd tell her stories as they sat around an old potbellied stove in the shop where he sold the things he made.

He had promised to carve something special for her for when she was older. However, sadly, he'd died when Gretel was only seven years old and Hansel was eight. Although she'd never gotten that special gift from him, she figured that carrying on the tradition of the carving craft in her family was *her* gift to her grandfather. Maybe she would find some good pieces of wood for new figures while out in the forest today, she thought as she turned to go.

Spotting the small basket full of assorted hair ribbons on the corner of her desk, she said, "Oops! Almost forgot." Pausing, she grabbed a handful of them and stuffed them into the pocket of her dress. Ribbons were another thing she never went hiking without.

Malorette and Odette were already waiting for her by the time she reached the stone walkway. She could tell they noticed her new hairstyle, but when they didn't mention it, she started to wonder if it looked bad or something. She hoped not.

When they all reached the first floor, the Steps immediately made for the castle exit.

"Wait! I thought we could get some breakfast before we start out?" Gretel suggested, pointing toward the Great Hall. "Hiking on an empty stomach is never a good idea."

Malorette arched an eyebrow. "You haven't eaten yet?"

"Well, no. I was busy packing stuff and —"

"We've already been to the Great Hall for breakfast," Odette huffily interrupted her. "We expected you to eat before we met!"

"Then you should have said so," Gretel couldn't resist saying.

Malorette frowned at her. "We need to get going. *Now*."

"Why? What's the rush?" asked Gretel. "Just how far away is this secret place anyway?"

"Shh! Tell the world, why don't you?" hissed Odette. She glanced around to remind her they could be overheard by any of the other students passing them in the hall. Then she explained vaguely, "It's a ways."

Lowering her voice, Gretel started backing away from them toward the Great Hall. "I'm starving. It'll just take me a few minutes to run into the Hall and get a few things to put in my backpack to eat along the way. Wait for me, okay?"

"Oh, all right." Malorette tapped her foot impatiently.

Odette rolled her eyes. "Meet us on the drawbridge. Make it fast."

Leaving the sour sisters to make their way out of the castle without her, Gretel rushed into the Great Hall. Just outside the serving area she stopped by the snacks table and grabbed several apples and oranges, and a couple of bags of trail mix (which was mostly walnuts, hazelnuts, and raisins). After stuffing the snacks into her backpack, she slung it over her shoulders again and started back out of the Hall.

She was almost to the door when she heard someone call her name. She wheeled around as Hansel and Jack came up to her. Jack's forehead was still bandaged, she noticed. He always seemed to heal quickly, though, so the bandage would probably come off in no time.

"Where are you going?" Hansel asked, gesturing toward her backpack and glancing down at her boots.

"Dancing," she said, joking around. Then she added casually, "Kidding. I'm just heading out for a morning hike."

Smiling his adorable dimpled smile, Jack asked, "By yourself?"

"Uh, yeah," Gretel lied.

Hansel lifted his brows, a sure sign he didn't believe her. But knowing he didn't trust Malorette and Odette, there was no way she would tell him she was going with them. And into Neverwood Forest of all places! She didn't relish having him warn her off and scold her, thank you very much. Especially not in front of Jack. If Malorette and Odette were telling the truth, this hike was a real opportunity. And if not, well, she would be on her guard.

"If you give us a few minutes, we'll put on our boots, too, and . . ." Hansel began.

Uh-oh. Time for a little more pushback. "I kind of feel like doing a hike alone right now. Okay? See you guys later," Gretel said quickly. As she shot away, she could feel two pairs of suspicious boy eyes boring into her back though.

"Hey," Jack called after her. "I like your new hair!" His voice wasn't all that loud, yet it seemed to fill the entire Hall. Heads turned to look at her.

He likes it! He likes it! After the way the stepsisters had ignored the new style, Gretel was extra thrilled by his compliment. She waved and smiled her thanks back at him. Of course, it wasn't like she could glue her hair back on if he *didn't* like it, so she was glad he did. Anyway, she didn't stop moving, for fear that Hansel would pipe up and insist on tagging along.

Once outside, she heard distant shouts coming from the Once Upon River. Glancing toward the sound, she saw that several boats filled with students were making their way over to Ice Island. Others already *on* the island were zooming around on skates. Most were heading for the new castle Snowflake had built after the collapse of her first one. It had lots of cool features like ice slides, ski jumps, and even a bobsled track with a smooth floor, walled straight sections, and banked curves.

For a moment Gretel found herself wishing she and Jack (and maybe Hansel, too) were heading for fun on Ice Island as well. But no, she had hiking and some important sleuth-ing to do!

Malorette and Odette were waiting for her at the far end of the Pink Castle drawbridge. "Took you long enough," Malorette complained when Gretel came up to them. Odette thrust the map from yesterday into Gretel's hands and the girls were off.

As they entered Neverwood Forest, Gretel tried to put on a brave face to hide her fear. But when a loud, piercing howl came from somewhere close by, she nearly jumped out of her skin. "Wh-what was th-that?" she asked shakily.

"Probably a wolf," Malorette said matter-of-factly. With a snide grin she added, "You're shivering. Not scared, are you?"

"N-no, not a bit," Gretel lied.

"Ha!" cackled Odette. "Then why are your eyes as big and worried as Mr. Hump-Dumpty's?" Their Grimm History egg-teacher had eyes as big as melons.

"I said I'm not scared," Gretel insisted. There was no way she was going to admit to the sisters how petrified she really was. "I was shivering because it's cold."

"Uh-huh," said Odette in a way that showed she didn't buy it. For some reason the sisters seemed totally unfazed by the forest's creepiness.

It *was* chilly here in the woods, though. The trees grew so thick they blocked out most of the sunlight. And the path was still damp from all the recent rain. Gretel thought about pulling her cloak from her backpack and putting it on, but didn't bother. She knew she'd warm up the more she hiked.

As they moved along, Gretel began to suspect that the two sisters must have been in Neverwood Forest before. Because they didn't look at the trail markers or seem to need the map or any directions from her. Did they really even need a guide at all? Maybe they were only *pretending* to need her help. But if so, why? It didn't make sense.

When they came to a T, the sisters went left before Gretel could even consult the map. It was as if they already knew which way to turn. And that made her even more suspicious about why they'd asked her to come.

Hearing a slithering sound, Gretel glanced down just in time to see a vine at the side of the trail shoot out and begin to wrap itself around one of her ankles. "Get off me!" she yelped, jumping around. As she shook her booted foot high in the air, the sisters stopped in the middle of the path and laughed uproariously. At the sound of their screechy cackles, the vine let go and crept away.

Gretel ran down the path past the sisters to get far away from that creeping vine. Then she stopped, her heart going a mile a minute. To calm herself, and because she was feeling hungry, she slipped off her backpack and took out an apple. "Want something?" she asked Malorette and Odette when they caught up.

"No, thanks," said Malorette.

"We had breakfast, remember?" Odette added.

Gretel shrugged, slipped the pack onto her shoulders, and then marched onward just ahead of the sisters. Turning her head over one shoulder, she munched her apple and tried to talk to them at the same time. "If oo change yer mindz, lemmee no. I brought pleny snacks for olive us." She'd probably never win them over as friends, but she could still set a good example by being kind.

"Uh, thanks," said Odette. She exchanged a sly look with her sister that Gretel had no idea how to interpret.

As the three girls hiked farther into the forest, they eventually veered off the well-beaten path they'd been following. There were lots of other paths branching off along the one they traveled. So to mark their way, Gretel stopped every now and then to tie one of the bright-colored hair ribbons she'd brought to a bush or a tree branch.

"Is that really necessary?" Malorette asked, watching her tie a blue one to a branch. "I mean, we've got the map. And you slow us down every time you stop."

"When hiking a new and unfamiliar trail, it's always

important to mark it," Gretel replied firmly. She shifted from foot to foot as she spoke, just in case any creepy vines were around, planning a sneak attack on her ankles. "That's why I always bring hair ribbons. Because we don't want to get lost, right? What if we strayed from the map accidentally and needed to retrace our steps? The ribbons will make finding our way back out a snap. We won't even need the map."

"But Mr. Hump-Dumpty doesn't want everyone to know about his secret place," objected Odette. "Your ribbons will lead them right to it."

"Not a problem," Gretel told her. "I always take down the ribbons on my return trip, so we'll do that on the way back to the Academy later."

"Great idea," Malorette exclaimed a little too exuberantly. She and Odette grinned at each other. Were they mocking her? Gretel wondered. *Whatever.* It was impossible to figure them out sometimes, but she really, really did hope they were telling the truth about the so-called secret destination they were heading for.

She munched trail mix as they all continued through the forest, and tried to keep her feelings of terror at bay whenever she heard strange noises, such as the thumps that came from behind them at regular intervals. It kind of sounded like someone was following them. Every time they stopped, the thumping stopped. But since Malorette and Odette didn't mention the sounds, she didn't either, for fear of being teased half to death about being a chicken.

Several times leafy tree branches grabbed at her hair or her gown or her backpack and she had to shake herself free, just as she'd done with the vine. She noticed that the vegetation left Malorette and Odette alone, however. Was that because the trees were more frightened of the evil sisters than the sisters were of them? Probably. Because the very next time she became entangled in a tree, Malorette narrowed her eyes at it and barked, "Let go of her this instant or I'll break off all of your branches!" Her threat was effective. The tree practically bent over backward to lift its branches high and away.

"So how much longer do you think it will take to get to Mr. Hump-Dumpty's secret place?" Gretel asked after they'd hiked for a couple of hours.

"How would we know?" Odette replied. "He told us about it, but we've never been there before."

"Can't you tell?" Malorette replied, gesturing toward the map Gretel held.

Gretel shook her head. "The map shows directions and landmarks but not the distances between them." After a pause, she asked, "Didn't Mr. Hump-Dumpty give you some idea of how long the trip is?"

"I think we've come about halfway," Odette replied shortly.

"But since we've never been there, we don't really know," said Malorette. "We're depending on you."

"I saw you heading into this forest yesterday before dinner, though," said Gretel, without thinking.

Suddenly, Malorette had a strange coughing fit and gazed meaningfully at her sister as if trying to wordlessly send her some message. As soon as she got her cough under control she said, "We'd . . . uh . . . actually intended to hike to Mr. Hump-Dumpty's secret place yesterday, only we decided we'd need an earlier start if we wanted to get back before dark."

"Yeah, and we also realized we needed a guide," Odette added.

"Oh, that explains it, I guess." Looking over her shoulder at the two girls, Gretel saw Odette elbow her sister and smirk. They were definitely up to something. Were they setting some kind of trap for her? When they'd passed her in the Bouquet Garden yesterday, she'd suspected they were going to meet Ms. Wicked. Or even Ludwig Grimm. But why would those two grown-ups be lurking so deep in this forest? She needed to find out what or who actually did lay ahead.

Trying to sound casual, she attempted to get some information out of her companions. "So some students think Ms. Wicked wound up in the Nothingterror when she escaped . . . uh . . . *left* the Academy. Think that's true?"

There was a moment of silence. Then Malorette said, "No clue."

Changing the subject, Odette reached out to Gretel. "Hand me your backpack. I'm hungry after all."

"Me too," Malorette agreed quickly.

Stopping, Gretel shrugged off her pack. "Here," she said handing it over to them. "Take whatever you like."

Malorette grabbed it and then pretended to stagger a bit under its weight. "Whoa! This thing is heavy." After digging her hand around in it, she took out an orange and began to peel it.

"Can I see the map?" Odette said after she'd helped herself to a handful of trail mix.

Gretel passed the map to her. After squinting at it for a few moments, Odette folded it up and put it in her pocket.

"Let's keep moving while we eat," said Malorette. "If we really are only halfway there, we've still got another couple of hours to go."

Gretel reached for her backpack, but Odette slipped its straps over her own shoulders. "I'll carry it for a while. You brought a bunch of supplies that we're all using, so it's not fair for you to have to carry this heavy thing the whole way. We can trade back in an hour."

"Thanks," Gretel said, surprised and pleased by this unexpected kindness. They'd only been hiking for another ten minutes or so when they came to a major fork in the trail. "I'd better take another look at the map," she said to Odette. "I can't remember if we turn right or left."

"Okay." Odette reached into her pocket. As her fingers felt around in it, a strange look came over her face. "Oh, no!" she exclaimed. "The map must have fallen out! I'll go back and look for it." She took off down the path the way they'd come.

"I'll go help her find it. Wait for us here," Malorette told Gretel.

"We really should all stay togeth —" Gretel started to say, but Malorette had already bounded away.

Oh, well, thought Gretel. The sisters couldn't possibly get lost with all the ribbons she'd left marking the way they'd come. And she was kind of tired after carrying that pack for most of the hike. She could use a break. She sank down on a fallen log at the side of the path to wait for their return.

7

Thump!

Hoot! Hoot! Gretel hunched her shoulders, her eyes darting nervously around the forest. It was filled with spooky sounds. Creaking trees, hooting owls, and howls that may or may not have come from wolves. And that thumping sound was back. It was probably some big bird that was flying around pecking at trees to look for bugs to eat. The noises hadn't bothered her too much until she was alone.

Where were Malorette and Odette? To bolster her courage while waiting for their return, she belted out her favorite nursery rhyme song. It was the one about her friends Jack and Jill:

> *"Jack and Jill went up the hill*
> *To fetch a pail of water;*
> *Jack fell down and broke his crown,*
> *And Jill came tumbling after."*

Despite the rhyme's dire words, the song was a jaunty one. And singing it in a loud voice helped to tune out some of those spooky sounds. She sang it a second time and then a third.

Suddenly, a loud squawk followed by a screech came from somewhere nearby. Gretel jerked a little and her hands began to tremble in her lap. She needed an activity to calm herself. Automatically, she reached into the pocket of her gown for her pocketknife, thinking she could find a nice piece of wood and carve something while waiting. But her knife wasn't there. *Oh, no!* She'd put it into her backpack instead of her pocket. And unfortunately, Odette had her backpack right now.

"Fudgenuts!" she exclaimed out loud. Feeling restless, she leaped up from the mossy log she'd been sitting on and began to pace back and forth in front of it. The damp ground seemed to suck at her boots. She started imagining beasts below the earth trying to drag her down to her doom. Yikes! She sat on the log again and drew up her knees, wrapping both arms around them.

What was taking those sisters so long? After at least fifteen minutes had gone by, she finally decided to go look for them.

She started back down the trail, but quickly got confused. Where were the ribbons she'd left on branches to mark their way back to the Academy? She didn't see a single one along the path. Had she made a wrong turn without realizing it? Unlike Red Riding Hood, her sense of direction was usually excellent, but Neverwood Forest was very dense. And all the trees were starting to look alike to her.

On the other hand, maybe she *was* on the right path. Birds could have taken the ribbons to build their nests. Gretel looked up into the branches of nearby trees to see if she could spot any nests with colorful ribbons wound through them. No luck.

"Malorette!" she called out. "Odette?" No answer.

A horrible suspicion began to creep over her. A suspicion that although she'd been determined to keep her wits about her, those sour sisters had *still* managed to trick her! They'd run off, leaving her alone in the woods without a map or her backpack. And even worse, maybe they'd removed the ribbons she'd used to mark their trail, making it nearly impossible for her to find her way out of the forest and back to GA. Talk about mean!

Gretel fought down the panicky feelings rising inside her. Maybe she was wrong and the two girls had already returned via some shortcut to the log where they'd told her to stay. She swung around and retraced her steps to the log. Maybe they'd be there, waiting for her.

But her gut was telling her that there were just two possibilities to explain what had happened. Either the sisters had changed their minds about showing her Mr. Hump-Dumpty's secret place after all and had looped around her to continue on ahead by themselves. Or else the secret place did not exist at all. And if there *was* no secret place, that would have to mean that Malorette and Odette had deliberately led her into these woods with the intention of abandoning her here.

A cold shiver ran down her spine. Why would they do that? Yes, they were evil, but even evil characters had reasons for what they did. Was it because they still thought she was a spy? She couldn't think of anything she'd seen or heard that made her a threat to them. It just didn't make sense!

Unfortunately, Gretel's gut feeling proved to be right. When she reached their meeting place, Malorette and Odette were not waiting for her. They had definitely dumped her. Unable to hold on to hope any longer, Gretel sank down on the fallen log. Tears leaked from the corners of her eyes and rolled down her cheeks. She should have listened to Hansel, she scolded herself as she angrily swiped at the tears. She had thought she could take care of herself, but she'd been wrong. Just look at what had happened!

Suddenly, she heard those weird thumping sounds again. Only this time they were much closer than before. Were the big pecking birds here to peck her to pieces now that she was alone and defenseless? Her throat seized up. But wait! Maybe it was just Malorette and Odette tramping back for her! She sprang up from the log and ran toward the sounds.

"Malorette!" she called out. "Odette! I'm here!" But neither girl answered.

The thumping sounds soon drew her into a small clearing. Confused, she turned in a circle, seeing no big birds. "No one here but me and my stupid imagination to scare me!" she muttered to herself. In an attempt to clear and calm her mind, she began to clomp in circles around the clearing. All at once she heard the sounds again. *Thump! Thump! Thump!* And now they were right behind her!

She whirled around. But again, there was nothing. Except . . . a stick lying on the ground a few feet away. She stepped over to it and picked it up. This was no ordinary, random stick. About a yard long, it was polished and smooth except for a couple of knots. And one end was curved like a handle.

"A walking stick!" she murmured, remembering the snazzy one Mr. Hump-Dumpty used like a cane as he walked.

This one didn't look exactly like his, but perhaps he had extras for outdoor hiking?

"Mr. Hump-Dumpty?" she called out hopefully. If his secret place really did exist, maybe it was nearby. Had he been on his way to visit it but dropped this stick in his hurry to hide when he heard someone coming? (That someone being *her*!) It was possible. That egg-teacher was even less brave than she was!

"Mr. Hump-Dumpty?" Gretel called out his name several times. But the egg-teacher didn't appear. He was terrified of just about everything, but not of a student like her. Since he didn't reply, he must not be here after all. Deeply disappointed and disheartened, she flung the stick away.

"What now?" she wondered aloud. Talking to herself helped make her feel less alone.

Considering the hollow, empty feeling in her stomach, she guessed it was well past lunchtime. All she'd had to eat that morning was an apple and some trail mix. She swallowed hard, feeling thirsty as well.

"I need to find food and water," she murmured. "If I still had my backpack, that wouldn't be a problem, of course. But those evil sisters left me with nothing! There's got to be a spring around here somewhere, though. Too bad Jack and Jill aren't here with their magic pail since it fills with water whenever they ask. Mmm. Water." She licked her lips.

Making it her goal to find a spring, Gretel set off through the forest again with renewed determination. As she walked, she listened for the telltale trickle of running water and looked for vegetation that was taller and healthier than the plants around it. Certain types of trees always grew near water. So she would keep an eye out for aspens, cedars, and willows. And for damp earth, too, although that might not be such a good clue since it had rained so much during the last few days and most of the ground was soggy.

Though still lost, she felt better now that she had a plan and a goal. However, she'd only been walking for a few minutes when she heard that thumping sound again. Her heart jumped into her throat. She whirled around but, as before, saw no one. "Who's there? Whoever you are, show yourself or stop following me!" she yelled.

Wait! There was that walking stick again. She'd tossed it away into some bushes before she set off, so how come it was lying just a few feet behind her now?

"Okay, this is just getting too weird!" she murmured.

Then something happened that was even weirder. The walking stick jumped upright and thumped toward her. All by itself!

Gretel stared at it, too stunned to move. When it reached her, the stick came to a stop. Still upright, it wobbled back and forth a little as if uncertain what to do next. Its behavior reminded her of another magical object she was well acquainted with — Red's *basket*. She gasped. A flicker of hope lit inside her — the first such flicker she'd felt since she'd realized once and for all that Malorette and Odette had ditched her.

Then she spoke to the stick, which was kind of a dumb thing to do unless ... "Are you my magic charm?" she asked it.

The stick didn't answer, but then, Gretel had never known of a magic charm that *could* talk. "Thump once for yes and twice for no," she told it.

Instead, the walking stick leaped into her hand. She laughed in delight. "I guess I'll take that as a yes."

8

Hansel

An uneasy feeling had come over Hansel as he'd watched Gretel leave the Great Hall to go off hiking by herself. Why hadn't she wanted Jack and him to go with her?

"Gretel's up to something," he murmured to Jack now as the two boys headed for the breakfast line.

"You always think people are up to something," said Jack, rolling his eyes. Then his gaze fell on a group of girls at one of the tables, who were giggling and whispering. "Come to think of it, around this school, they usually are up to something!"

"It's just that she's been acting bristly lately. Secretive, even," Hansel went on. She used to tell him everything. Now, not so much. It was like she was mad at him all the time.

"She thinks you're too bossy," Jack informed him.

"What?" Hansel sputtered as he and Jack joined the breakfast line. "Did she tell you that?"

"No, just a guess," said Jack, shrugging.

Bossy? Me? thought Hansel. Didn't Gretel know he was only watching out for her and trying to keep her safe? What was so wrong with that? He was her big brother, after all. That's what big brothers did!

He and Jack inched along in line, standing behind some of the guys, including Prince Awesome and Prince Prince. Everybody was talking about the rain and how swampy everything was outside, but Hansel tuned them out.

He felt kind of grouchy and unsettled. For one thing, he wasn't sure he liked Gretel's new haircut. He'd noticed the change, of course. But unlike Jack, he hadn't commented on it. The absence of her long braid made her look . . . well . . . more grown up. Is that why she'd cut it off? Because she wanted to appear older? Like someone who didn't need her big brother to keep an eye on her? *Hmm.* It was something to think about. He heaved a sigh. She used to be easy to figure out. Lately, though, it was hard to guess what was going on inside his sister's head.

Like now. What was she hiding? He should've asked her which way she was going when he had the chance. It wasn't smart to hike alone. He hoped she would at least stick to one of the trails they knew well.

"Save me a place in line, okay?" Hansel said to Jack. Then before Jack could reply, he zipped over to one of the

Hall's tall diamond-paned windows that looked out across the Once Upon River.

Craning his neck to the left, he saw Malorette and Odette standing at the far end of the Pink Castle drawbridge. *Bleah!* Those horrid girls again?

Seconds later, he saw his sister come out onto the drawbridge. She paused briefly to look out toward Ice Island before continuing across the bridge. He could see that Malorette and Odette were watching her. Sort of like spiders waiting for a fly to come into their web.

He expected her to walk right by them as anyone with half a brain would do. Instead, as his sister went up to them, they said something to her and she stopped. Then, for some reason, Odette thrust a piece of paper into Gretel's hand. *Huh?* He watched his sister study the paper for a minute. And then, much to his astonishment, the three girls walked off together. In the direction of Neverwood Forest, no less!

What in Grimmlandia was going on? Did Malorette and Odette have some kind of hold over his sister? Is that why she'd gone off with them?

Hansel's first instinct was to bolt from the Great Hall and run after the girls. Whipping around to do just that, he bumped into Jack. He'd apparently already gone through the line because he was now precariously balancing two breakfast trays, one on the palm of each hand.

"Whoa! Help! Quick!" Jack yelled, eyeing the tilting trays with concern. "Grab one before they both drop!"

Hansel rescued one of the trays in the nick of time, while Jack managed to cling to the other. *Mmm.* Something smelled grimmyummy. There was a big bowl of Hagscorch's delicious nine-day-old pease porridge on each tray. And also a couple of hot cross buns.

"Thanks," he mumbled to Jack. By the time he looked outside again, the girls were already entering the forest. He'd never catch them now.

"Whatcha looking at?" Jack asked, leaning over to gaze out the window, too. Before Hansel could reply, Jack did a double take. The single tray he was still holding tilted to one side and the porridge almost slid right off. Hansel caught it at the last minute and set it back on the tray.

Jack never even noticed that a disaster had almost occurred. "Hey! What's Gretel doing going into Neverwood Forest with Malorette and Odette?" he said, actually sounding worried for once.

"Good question." Hansel frowned. As they set their trays down on the nearest table, he took a step toward the exit. "I'm going to go follow them."

Jack wrinkled his bandaged forehead. "Wait. You sure that's a good idea?"

"What do you mean?" Hansel asked in surprise.

"What I mean, Mr. Bossy Bro, is would Gretel want you to do that?" asked Jack. "You know she's just going to get mad at you for following her around like you think she can't take care of herself. She's a strong hiker. Maybe you should just wait till she gets back to talk to her."

Hansel opened his mouth to argue that it was his responsibility to look after Gretel even if she might not see it that way, but then he closed it. Because he'd remembered her new, more grown-up, haircut. And also how she'd so obviously not wanted Jack and him to go hiking with her.

She must've been planning to meet Malorette and Odette all along, he realized. And she'd lied about it because she knew how he felt about those two. Well, as hard as it was for him, he'd respect her wishes, he decided. This time anyway.

"Okay," he told Jack, sitting down across from him at last. "Let's eat."

Hansel picked up a hot cross bun from his plate. He stared at it warily. Although they tasted great, the buns were not his favorite. They were grumpy and crosspatchy and always trying to talk you out of eating them. As he started to bite into the bun, it complained, "Wait! You're making a mistake!"

A mistake eating it, the bun meant. But, thinking of Gretel, Hansel couldn't help wondering if his *real* mistake was in not going after her. Feeling as grumpy as the bun, he murmured, "Too bad," and shoved it into his mouth.

9

Sticking It Out

Gretel curled her fingers around the walking stick's handle. It fitted itself comfortably in her hand. Just holding on to the stick somehow made her feel calmer and braver. "So can you lead me out of here?" she asked it. No response.

Sometimes charms came with printed instructions that at least hinted at how the charm worked. This had been the case with Red's basket. When she had opened its lid, she'd found a piece of vellum paper inside. The words *A tisket, a tasket* had been written on it, followed by six fill-in-the-blank spaces. That clue had helped Red figure out how to phrase her commands to make the basket's magic work.

And Snow White's magic charm, a tiara that could turn her invisible, had come with a riddle. Snow had shared it with everyone, and Gretel could still remember it:

"Riding on high,
I trick the eye.

If you wish to fool,
Press my center jewel.
Where once was something
will appear nothing."

It hadn't taken Snow long to figure out what the riddle meant. To make her tiara work, she only needed to set it atop her head and press the turquoise jewel on its center front.

"So what makes you tick, stick?" Gretel asked. "I don't see a card or note anywhere. Of course, that isn't unusual. Not all magic charms come with instructions. Snowflake's wand didn't. Neither did Rapunzel's magic comb or Rose's magic hairpin. But if you are my charm, a few hints about how you work would really be helpful."

She waited, but no hints came.

"Well, I guess it's up to me to figure out what you can do," Gretel mused, trying not to feel discouraged. "I don't suppose you could fetch me some food and water?" But still the walking stick didn't react, not even a jiggle.

"So does that mean fetching isn't something you can do? Just asking because Red's basket can fetch snacks. But come to think of it, a basket has a place to carry them in and you don't."

Knowing that charms often responded to rhyme, she

decided to try something different. Rephrasing her request, she said, "Hey, stick. I'm in the mood for food."

To her surprise, the walking stick gave an abrupt, hard jerk. And then she found herself being propelled forward as it began to thump through the forest again, with her hand attached to its handle.

"Whoa! You sure can move fast when you want to," Gretel told it as she held on tight and breathlessly ran to keep up. "Are you leading me back to the Academy? That would be perfect. There's food and water there, and my bed. And two sisters I'd like you to thump. Well, I don't *really* mean that. If they are there, I'll just give them a very big piece of my mind!"

She turned her head this way and that, all the while trying to keep up with the stick. "Hey, I'm not doubting you or anything, but I don't recognize this part of the forest. Are you sure you're going the right way?"

She didn't expect an answer and didn't get one. The walking stick was probably just taking her on a different (and, hopefully, quicker) route through the woods to GA.

When they came to a really dense thicket of bushes and brambles, the stick raised its tip and swished back and forth over the bushes. At once they magically parted to create a path where none had been before, allowing Gretel to walk through easily.

"Wow. Good work," she praised her probably-charm. "You sure know how to blaze a trail!"

Seemingly delighted at her compliment, the stick leaped free for a moment to twirl in the air like a baton. Then it settled under her hand again and went back to work, parting the bushes and guiding her forward. And a minute later, when a creeping vine made a grab for her ankle, the stick gave it a sharp rap, which caused the vine to quickly withdraw.

"Thanks," Gretel told the stick.

They'd been walking for at least an hour, when she finally saw a faint light in the distance. Was it the Academy? Unlikely. Her surroundings were completely unfamiliar.

"Where in Grimmlandia are we?" she asked her stick as it continued to draw her forward. But as usual, it didn't answer.

All of a sudden, they broke free of the thick group of trees they'd been traveling through. A few steps later, she halted in her tracks and so did her stick. Because it was impossible to go any farther. They were facing a wall. A wall that was blocking their way out of this end of the forest. It was impossibly tall and seemed to extend as high as the clouds, running parallel to the tree line and stretching farther than she could see to the left and right. Afternoon sun glinted off it, making it appear to be made of slippery frosted glass.

Gretel gasped as realization struck. "I don't believe it! This must be *the* Wall!" Then in case her stick needed further explanation, she added, "The magical wall that surrounds Grimmlandia and keeps it safe from the Dark Nothingterror where Barbarians and Dastardlies roam." As far as she knew, Rose was the only other student at the Academy who had ever actually seen the Wall.

As her eyes traveled along its smooth expanse, she spied a hill in front of it not far away. The light she'd noticed earlier was shining from the window of a cottage that sat at the very top of the hill. She could see the silhouette of someone in the window, and that someone appeared to be stirring a pot. Suddenly, Gretel was quaking in her hiking boots. Because that someone also happened to be wearing a tall pointy hat — the kind that witches wore.

Without warning, Gretel's stick zoomed off for the hill, pulling her with it as it began to climb.

"Maybe we could find food and water somewhere else?" she suggested as it tugged her upward. But her stick didn't turn around *or* slow down. Well, if her magic charm was convinced that the cottage was a safe place to go, then it *must* be safe.

Besides, she was *really, really* hungry. So hungry that she didn't really care right now if the person inside was a witch, as long as she gave Gretel something to eat. Maybe there would be something tasty in that pot the witch stirred.

As she drew closer to the top of the hill, Gretel got a better view of the cottage. Her mouth dropped in surprise. It looked like a giant copy of one of Mistress Hagscorch's gingerbread houses, complete with candy decorations such as gumdrops and licorice sticks, lollipops and jelly beans!

"Grimmalicious!" Gretel wrapped her arms around her walking stick and hugged it. "I'm sorry I ever doubted you. You're the best!" she exclaimed. "Thank you, thank you, thank you!"

She reached out to knock on the door, which had a big round blue jawbreaker for its knob. *But wait*, she thought, drawing her hand back. Maybe she didn't need to come face-to-face with the witch or whoever the potentially scary person living inside the yummy-looking pink-frosted cottage was. She could just take a bite (or maybe two or three or ten) to eat of this cottage and continue on her way.

Keeping well away from the windows, which appeared to be made of transparent sugar, she stood on her tiptoes and reached up. As carefully and quietly as possible, she broke off a single tile from the white-frosted gingerbread roof. *Crack!*

A little squeak of pleasure escaped her when she took her first bite. Except for Mistress Hagscorch's gingerbread house cookies, it was the most delicious thing she'd ever tasted.

Suddenly, a voice from inside the cottage called out. "Nibble, nibble. Is that a mouse? Nibbling, nibbling at my house?"

Gretel froze, roof tile cookie in hand. Did the witch expect a reply? Maybe the mice around here were enchanted ones that spoke. It was certainly possible since Grimmlandia was full of magical creatures. If the witch thought a mouse was eating her house, would she come after it, though?

Unsure what to do, Gretel finally blurted out, "*Wooooo.* Not a mouse. Oooonly the wind blowing doooown the chimney."

But apparently neither the mice nor the winds in this magical place could speak, and the witch wasn't fooled. Before Gretel could turn and run, the door was thrust open and an old woman with straggly white hair appeared in the doorway. Aside from the fact that she had one yellow eye and one green one, she was practically the spitting image of Mistress *Scary*scorch, and most assuredly a witch.

Instantly, Gretel's walking stick slipped from her fingers and flew into the witch's hand. "My stick!" The witch cackled with delight. "I lost it when I was walking in the woods yesterday. I'm so happy you found it for me!"

10

A Proper Meal

"*Your* stick?" Gretel said in surprise. Her shoulders sagged with disappointment. She'd been so sure the walking stick was her magical charm. But of course it made just as much sense, maybe even more, that the stick actually belonged to this witch. That must be why it had brought Gretel here. It hadn't been following her command to find food after all. It had simply been heading for home and, for some reason, had decided to bring her along.

"Come in, come in," the witch urged. Glancing at the piece of roof cookie Gretel still held, she added, "Let me give you a *proper* meal. A reward for bringing me back my precious walking stick."

"Uh, thanks," said Gretel, belatedly slipping the cookie into her pocket to hide it. "But I really do need to get going." Frankly, the thought of entering the witch's house terrified her even more than spending the night (if it should come to that) lost in Neverwood Forest.

"Nonsense," said the witch. She opened her door wider and a scrumptious smell of apples and cinnamon wafted out. "I just stirred up some batter and made a big apple pancake. You can share it with me."

Gretel hesitated. That pancake really did smell good. And there was no reason to assume this witch was evil. Her actions so far had been kind, and good witches *did* exist. "Are you a good witch or a bad witch?" she blurted out. The words just slipped from her mouth without warning.

The woman gave a cackle of laughter, as if Gretel had just told the funniest joke ever. "Don't be silly. Just call me Emelda. Now, come inside and eat."

Feeling relieved by the woman's response, since it seemed to suggest that maybe she wasn't a witch at all, Gretel gave in to her hunger pangs. Summoning up her courage, she stepped inside the cottage. It was warm and cozy and simply furnished with a small wooden table and chairs, a tiny stove, and white-painted cupboards with a cute, green leafy border painted along their sides and tops.

"Please sit down," her host said, gesturing toward the chairs around the table. There were three of them, with pretty flowered cushions on their seats. Gretel pulled out one of the chairs and sat. Her feet were a little sore from so much walking, so she unlaced her boots and kicked them off beneath the table. *Ahh. That's better*, she thought as she stretched out her legs and stocking feet.

"What were you doing in the forest anyway?" Emelda asked as she set plates and forks and a pitcher of maple syrup on the table. After cutting up the large apple pancake, she slid one slice onto Gretel's plate. Then she went back for two glasses and a big jug of milk before sitting down to eat.

Gretel poured a generous amount of syrup over her pancake. It was puffy, with a center of sliced baked apples. "I was out hiking," she said before taking a huge bite of it. "Mmm. Delicious!" she murmured. Of course food always tasted particularly good to her after hiking when she was really and truly hungry.

The woman cocked her head. "You went hiking out in the forest all by yourself?"

"Well, I started out with two other girls from Grimm Academy," Gretel told her as she forked up another bite of pancake. "But we got . . . uh . . . *separated*. And then I couldn't find them." She wasn't sure why she didn't tell the woman the truth. That Malorette and Odette had deliberately left her alone in Neverwood Forest. Maybe because the fact that the girls had ditched her made her sound really pathetic . . . and super dumb for trusting them!

For a split second, she thought she saw a sly smile flit across the woman's face. But she immediately dismissed this as a trick of the flickering light that was coming from a candle burning on the table. In a voice oozing with concern, the woman said, "How awful! But isn't it lucky that my stick found you and brought you here?"

"It sure was," Gretel agreed. "One of my friends at the Academy has been here to the Wall before," she added as she finished her pancake wedge. "But she never mentioned seeing a gingerbread cottage."

"Another slice?" Emelda asked, gesturing at the rest of the pancake. It was only half-gone. When Gretel nodded and held out her plate, the woman slid another piece onto it. "You know that the Wall completely surrounds Grimmlandia," she told Gretel. "I'm guessing your friend must have visited a different part of it."

"Yeah, guess so." Gretel gazed around as she poured syrup on her second piece of pancake. "You know what? This cottage looks just like these three-dimensional gingerbread cookies that Mistress Hagscorch makes — only much bigger, of course."

Emelda raised an eyebrow.

"Mistress Hagscorch is the Academy's cook," Gretel explained.

"And is she a good cook?" Emelda asked casually.

"The best!" Gretel enthused.

At this, a frown tugged at the corners of Emelda's mouth, and the point of her witch hat seemed to stand up pointier.

Uh-oh, thought Gretel. *For some strange reason this woman is acting jealous of Mistress Hagscorch's cooking skills!*

"But you're a great cook, too!" she exclaimed quickly. "This apple pancake is the best I've ever eaten!" Of course, she didn't add that this was the very first one she'd ever tasted. Mistress Hagscorch had never made apple pancakes for them at school!

The woman's frown disappeared. "Why, thank you," she said. "I do rather pride myself on my cooking abilities. In fact, I once applied for the job of Academy cook myself." Her frown crept back. "But your principal hired *that other woman*."

"Oh," said Gretel. Well, that explained the jealousy. She must have been really disappointed when Mistress Hagscorch got the job instead of her. "So did you decide to build your cottage from gingerbread and candy because you like to bake?" she asked. Being careful not to spill, she poured herself a tall glass of milk and then gulped it down.

"Not at all," answered Emelda as she refilled Gretel's glass with more milk. "I wanted to build from wood, but you know what the trees in Neverwood Forest are like. Whenever I tried to chop one down, its branches knocked my ax from my hands."

Having had some experience with those trees, Gretel totally understood. On the other hand, if she were a tree, she wouldn't want to be chopped down to make a house either.

"And the stones were even worse," the woman went on. "They threw themselves at me when I tried to gather them up."

"Yikes," said Gretel after draining the second glass of milk. "I can see why you decided to use gingerbread. But isn't it scary living so close to the Wall?"

Emelda shrugged. "Not really. Why would it be?"

"Well, because of the Barbarians and Dastardlies who live on the other side of it in the Dark Nothingterror," Gretel said in surprise.

"Oh, those," the woman said dismissively. "They howl a lot, especially at night, but I just throw them a few treats and that calms them down for a while."

"Really?" Gretel thought for a moment. "But the Wall is so *tall*. How do you toss the treats high enough to go over —"

"Let's talk about you," her host interrupted, abruptly changing the subject. "You haven't yet told me your name, and . . ."

"Gretel."

Emelda smiled. "Now, Gretel, I'm concerned that those girls you got . . . um . . . separated from could still be wandering around in the woods, trying to find you." She paused. "I hope you left word with someone else that you were going hiking in the forest?"

Gretel's cheeks reddened in embarrassment. "I should have told my older brother, Hansel, but I didn't." She refrained from adding that Malorette and Odette were probably back at the Academy by now and unlikely to tell anyone that they'd purposely abandoned her in Neverwood Forest.

"Oh, that's too bad," said Emelda. But strangely, her voice sounded more cheerful than sympathetic.

Her stomach full at last, Gretel rose from the table. "Thanks for the food, but I'd really better be going if I want to reach the Academy before dark." She just wished she knew how she would find her way back. She'd counted on her magic charm . . . um . . . this woman's walking stick to lead her out of the woods.

As if reading her mind, her host jumped up from the table, too. "It's much too late for you to return to the Academy tonight. You must stay here instead." Then she added, "I have a crystal ball. I'll use it to let Principal R know you're safe. And I'll find out if those other girls made it back." A smile played at her lips as she asked, "What did you say their names were?"

Gretel yawned. She couldn't remember when she'd last felt so tired. "I didn't say. But Malorette and Odette." She yawned again. "They're sisters."

A smile flashed across the woman's face again. "You're exhausted. And no wonder after the day you've had." She took Gretel's arm. "Let's get you to bed, and then I'll contact the school."

Gretel tried to protest that she was fine, but she was just *sooo* sleepy. Besides, her host had been nothing but kind, so where was the harm in spending the night? Her resistance crumbled completely when the woman led her into a cute little bedroom with lollipop-patterned wallpaper and an adorable small bed with a comforter as puffy and pink as cotton candy.

"Sweet dreams," Emelda called from the doorway. And then she closed the door softly behind her. Without bothering to take off her clothes — she had no pj's to change into, anyway — Gretel climbed into the bed, pulled the heavenly soft comforter up to her chin, and was instantly fast asleep.

But during the night, she roused briefly, thinking she heard a commotion somewhere inside the cottage. And raised voices, the witch's and . . . *Hansel*? But what would he be doing here? Deciding she must be dreaming, she rolled over, snuggled under the pink comforter, and fell back into an even deeper slumber. The Barbarians and Dastardlies beyond the Wall could have howled up a storm, but she was so soundly asleep, there was no way she would have heard them that night.

11

Hansel

"I still don't get why Gretel would go traipsing around in Neverwood Forest with those two abominable sisters," Hansel said to Jack that Saturday morning.

Breakfast was over and both the boys were taking the stairs up to their room in Onyx Tower. Even though Hansel had seen the wisdom in staying put at the Academy till his sister returned, and she'd only been out hiking with Malorette and Odette for about an hour, he couldn't stop thinking that something was very wrong.

"*Traipsing? Abominable?*" Jack repeated in a teasing tone. "Has anyone ever told you that you have a grimm-awesome vocabulary?"

Hansel grinned. He *was* a bit of a word nut. He loved dictionaries and thesauruses almost as much as he loved to hike. "Um, yeah. *You've* told me. Innumerable times, in fact," he said, using another big word. Sure he knew ordinary words, but unusual or complicated ones were more fun to say. In his opinion anyway.

It was kind of a standing joke among Jack, Jill, and Gretel that Hansel often offered definitions of big words he'd used, even if others already knew what they meant. Knowing that Jack would now be waiting for explanations, he supplied them. "*Traipsing*: to walk around aimlessly. *Abominable*: obnoxious, loathsome, despicable, diabolical, detestable."

At this, Jack started laughing so hard he almost fell over. "Ha-ha-ha! Tell me what you *really* think of those sisters, why don't you?"

Could someone get hurt from laughing too hard? Hansel decided not to define *innumerable* for fear Jack might actually injure himself.

By the time they reached the fifth-floor landing, Jack had calmed down and the boys were soon pushing aside the black-and-white-striped curtain that served as the door to their shared alcove. Jack went straight to the armoire at the foot of his high bed. He grabbed his jacket and slipped it on.

"Going somewhere?" Hansel asked.

Jack nodded. "Skating. Jill and I are heading over to Ice Island." He looped a long knitted yellow scarf around his neck. "Want to come?"

Hansel shook his head no. "Thanks, but I think I'll stay here and study." He pulled out his desk chair and straddled it to face Jack. "We've got that test in Grimm History coming up."

"Dude, today's Saturday!" exclaimed Jack. "The test isn't till Wednesday!"

"I know," said Hansel. "But . . ."

Jack grinned and finished his sentence for him. ". . . you don't like leaving things till the last minute. You like being well prepared. Yeah, I know. Me, on the other hand? I don't study until I absolutely have to!" He pulled a black stocking cap over his blond curls. "If you change your mind, meet us on the island. If not, I'll catch you at lunch and tell you all about the fun you missed."

Having already turned to work at his desk, Hansel waved and replied over one shoulder, "Okay, see you." Seconds later, remembering some words of advice he'd wanted to impart before Jack left, he jumped up again. Hurrying over to their curtain door, he poked his head out.

"And don't break any bones! No doing triple jumps or other insanely dangerous stuff!" he called out. But by then, Jack was out of sight and probably too far away to hear the cautions.

Some of the guys hanging out in the common area at the center of the dorm overheard him and laughed. "Hey!

Who are you, Mr. Hump-Dumpty? Maybe you should get a whistle like his, too," joked Prince Perfect. Leave it to him to say something rather mean. Despite his name, that prince was far from being perfectly kind.

But was he right? Hansel couldn't help wondering as he ducked back into his dorm room. *Did* he sound like Mr. Hump-Dumpty? Lately that egg-teacher had made it his business to be out on the ice on weekends and after school, shouting warnings to students: *"Not so close to the edge of the ice! Everybody skate left till I call to change direction! No speeding!"* Whenever someone broke his rules, he'd sound the loud whistle he'd gotten from Coach Candlestick.

Hansel plunked back down at his desk. Well, too bad. He'd rather annoy his friends with warnings than have them get hurt and then later regret that he hadn't cautioned them against trouble.

He'd told Jack the truth about wanting to get a head start on preparing for the history test. But he also hoped that studying would distract him from worrying about Gretel. And all the terrifying things in Neverwood Forest that might try to get her.

On top of his desk he found his Grimm Academy Handbook. He reached out with an index finger and pushed the oval GA logo on the front of it. "Grimm History of Barbarians and Dastardlies," he told the Handbook. You had to make clear what subject you wanted to read about before opening the Handbook, because it would change its text to reflect whatever class you were in.

Flipping to the chapters that the test would be covering, he began to review them. Unfortunately, the material included stuff about the many terrifying creatures that lurked just outside of Neverwood Forest in the Dark Nothingterror, including gigantic Dastardlies, which had but a single eye in the middle of their huge foreheads. His tension built as he memorized their names and descriptions.

This kind of studying was *not* helping him to worry less. Exactly the opposite! Every twenty minutes or so, concern about Gretel pricked him like the tip of a sword. Each time it happened, he'd jump up and go to the window between his and Jack's beds to look outside, hoping to spot her returning to the Academy. Nope. Finally, when it was time for lunch, he tossed his book aside and made his way downstairs.

As he entered the Great Hall, he quickly scanned every face. No Gretel. And no sign of the vile sisters she'd gone off with, either. He'd just sat at a table when Jack plopped down his tray, too, and slid onto the bench beside him. "The skating was grimmtastic! You missed out," he announced.

Hansel shot him a wicked grin. "So? How many times?"

Jack chuckled, knowing what he was asking. "Four. I only fell four times. No harm done, though. The hard part is getting back up on that slippery stuff."

The boys were soon joined by some of their other friends, including Prince Awesome, Prince Prince, Prince Knightly, and Prince Dragonbreath. There were a lot of princes at Grimm Academy. And princesses, too!

Talk at the table quickly turned to some of the guys' favorite subjects: jousting, catapulting, and masketball. The latter was a game played by two teams, in which players wore masks and shot balls through hoops. Hansel joined in the talk, though as sports went, he preferred hiking to every other kind of exercise.

Lunch was almost at an end when Jack gave him a nudge with his elbow. "Look who just walked in," he said, gesturing with his fork toward the Pink Castle end of the Great Hall.

Hansel looked up in time to see Malorette and Odette making their way to the lunch line. Gretel wasn't with them. He jumped up from the table, muttering, "Be right back."

Jack leaped up, too. "Not so fast, buddy. If you're going over there, I'm coming, too."

The boys marched right over to the girls. "Where's Gretel?" Hansel demanded as Malorette and Odette got their trays.

A worried look flashed between the sisters, but then Malorette curled her lip snarkily. "How would we know? She's *your* sister. Can't *you* keep track of her?" She and Odette moved to the lunch counter and held out their trays to Mistress Hagscorch.

The boys followed them. "We saw Gretel go off with you. Saw you heading toward Neverwood Forest," accused Hansel.

"I don't know what you're talking about." Odette smirked. "Maybe your eyes were playing a trick on you."

"We *both* saw her, though," Jack emphasized.

From the corner of his eye, Hansel noticed that Mistress Hagscorch had paused, plates of food in hand, to listen in on their conversation.

Suddenly, and without warning, Jack swooped toward Odette and grabbed something that was dangling from the pocket of her gown. A red ribbon. As he pulled on its end, it tumbled out, bringing a whole ball of other ribbons in various colors with it.

"Aha!" said Jack, holding them up in his fist. "I recognize these! They're Gretel's hair ribbons! She doesn't just wear them in her hair, either. She uses them to mark trails, too!"

Odette laughed nervously, then tried to bluff it out. "Okay. So the ribbons are hers." She glanced from him to

Hansel, adding, "We wanted a trail guide and you told us Gretel was good at following maps, remember?"

She took a bowl of go fish soup from Mistress Hagscorch. It was a weird sort of soup that had either tasty or strange surprises inside it. You never knew what they would be until you dipped your spoon in.

Hansel nodded reluctantly. "Yeah, but —"

"So we asked Gretel to help us," interrupted Malorette. "Then, to see if she was really as good as you and Jack said she was, we decided to play a little trick on her."

Odette snickered. "Yeah, we sneaked off. And we took down those ribbons as we walked back to the Academy to see if she could find her way back without them."

Jack's jaw dropped. "You did what?"

"She still has the map, though, right?" Hansel asked quickly. With the map she'd be able to find her way back. In fact, she might show up here any minute.

"Well . . . the thing is, we sort of . . . um . . . *lost* the map," said Malorette. The sly look she exchanged with her sister convinced Hansel she was lying. But before he could say anything more, Mistress Hagscorch, who had been quiet until now, practically exploded.

Wham! She banged the bowls of soup she was holding down onto the serving counter so hard that the soup sloshed. "You left that girl alone in the middle of Neverwood Forest?"

she cried out, glaring at the two sisters. Other students reached out around them in line and took the bowls of soup, then fled from the trouble they sensed brewing and went out into the dining area.

"Something fishy is going on here. And I don't just mean my go fish soup," the cook declared, wagging her big soup ladle at the sisters. "I suspect what you did is somehow linked to what my sister, Emelda, told me when we spoke by crystal ball last night." At the mention of Hagscorch's sister, Malorette and Odette turned a little pale.

Hansel hadn't even known Mistress Hagscorch *had* a sister. But why would he? Students didn't usually know that kind of stuff about school staff. "What did your sister say?" he asked the cook, more worried than ever now.

"That she was in cahoots with these two on some plan that — if it worked — would alter the course of Grimmlandia history and advance her status in E.V.I.L." After a pause, she added, "Emelda is given to exaggeration. She's always scheming about one thing or another and nothing ever comes of it, so I didn't give it much mind. Maybe I should have!"

Jack stepped closer to Malorette and Odette and gave them the stink eye. "Tell us what the plan was!"

The sisters exchanged another look. "Plan? We don't know anything about a plan," said Malorette.

"And we've never met anyone named Emelda, either," insisted Odette.

Bam! Mistress Hagscorch set more bowls of go fish soup on trays, and students continued quietly taking them. Stepping around the unfolding drama, they rushed off as fast as they could.

The cook's yellow eyes narrowed as she stared at the two girls. "Is that right, *dearies*? If you don't have any more information to offer, then you're not very useful to us, are you?" She reached over the counter with both clawed hands and pinched their cheeks. "But there's another way you could help. You see, I'm thinking of trying out a new recipe called sister stew," she told them, her eyes glinting with mischief. "And what I could really use is two tasty ingredients about your size."

Instant panic filled the sisters' faces. "Okay, wait, I just remembered. We *do* know Emelda," Malorette blurted all in a rush. "We talked to her by crystal ball yesterday, too. But the only thing we know about that plan of hers is that it has something to do with freeing Ms. Wicked from the Dark Nothingterror."

"Our job was to bring Gretel to the center of the forest," Odette hurried to explain. "Emelda had cooked up some scheme for getting her the rest of the way to her cottage. I bet Gretel's there now all safe and cozy!" Keeping a worried eye on Hagscorch, she pulled a map from her boot and held it out to Hansel.

"Oh, hey, look what Odette found. I thought we'd lost it," Malorette said weakly. She was obviously fibbing again to cover up her lie about having lost this very map.

Meanwhile, Mistress Hagscorch began dishing up soup as fast as she could, since the students in line behind the sisters and the two boys had begun getting impatient. She glanced over the counter at the map, then nodded at the boys. "Looks right," she told them.

While Hansel was studying it, Malorette and Odette silently fled the Hall. "There's no time to lose," he exclaimed a moment later. "I'm going after Gretel!"

Jack bounded after him as he ran off. "Wait for me!"

"I can't believe you recognized those ribbons as my sister's," Hansel called over his shoulder as he and Jack raced through the Great Hall to the Pink Castle side of the Academy. "What guy notices hair ribbons?"

Jack's face turned as red as the ribbon he'd first spied dangling from Odette's pocket. "I don't know. I notice lots of things."

Hmm, thought Hansel. It seemed to him that Jack noticed stuff about Gretel that no one else did. Well, he guessed it would be okay if Jack *like*-liked his sister. He wondered if she liked Jack back, though. As more than just a friend.

After clattering down a short flight of stairs, they pushed through the doors to the outside. They had just started across the drawbridge when Jack stumbled over his own feet. "Ow!" he yelped. "My ankle! I think I sprained it."

Hansel hesitated, looking back at him.

"Go!" Jack told him, waving him on. "I'll be okay. It's Gretel you need to rescue!"

Hansel nodded. Then he took off for Neverwood Forest.

12

Hansel

Hansel entered the forest alone. This place was so grimmcreepy it instantly gave him goosebumps. Was following the map he held a good idea? He wished he knew if Gretel really *was* at Hagscorch's sister's place or lost somewhere among these trees. Still, what choice did he have? Whether his sister knew it or not, she was in danger. He needed to find her, and this map was the sole clue he had to her whereabouts.

He was only about a hundred yards into the forest when he came across a bright-blue backpack. It was Gretel's! His heart began pumping harder. He unzipped its pockets to look inside and even turned the backpack upside down and shook it.

"Empty," he muttered in frustration. None of the usual snacks and supplies Gretel carried were in it. Speaking of supplies, he hadn't brought any himself. No water. No food.

No nothing. It was a rookie hiking mistake. But he couldn't take time to go back.

"Guess I'll have to hope I find a freshwater spring or some fruit. Or that I get to that cottage before I get hungry or thirsty. Fingers crossed," he said. Then he rolled his eyes, realizing that he was talking to himself like a crazy person. It was the forest's fault, he decided. Talking out loud was the only way to keep himself calm in here. Well, calm*er*, anyway.

Remembering the hair ribbons that had been stuffed in Odette's pocket, he guessed that she and Malorette had somehow convinced Gretel to let them have the backpack. Before they'd tricked her and run off with it, that is. Then, when they'd realized that he and Gretel's friends would recognize the pack as hers, the beastly sisters had ditched it here just before they reached the Academy.

Hansel slid the straps of the backpack over his shoulders and hiked on. He'd been in Neverwood Forest a few times before. Though he usually avoided coming here, his friend Wolfgang, who could shape-shift into a wolf, liked this forest. Sometimes, Hansel and the other guys at GA went hiking here with him, though it wasn't their favorite area by far.

Neverwood was full of sounds — the wind in the trees, the crunch underfoot of fallen pinecones and twigs, birdsong, the scurrying of small animals. Those were pleasant sounds. But there were also spooky sounds that Hansel couldn't identify so readily — howls and weird creaking noises, for example. He did his best to ignore those. And when creeping vines and grabby branches reached out to tug at his arms and legs, he fought them off.

From time to time, he checked the map to make sure he was heading in the right direction. After a couple of hours had passed, he realized he still had a long way to go. So he picked up his pace until he was almost jogging. Even so, the sun was setting when he finally reached the edge of the forest and caught a glimpse of the Wall and the cottage at the top of the hill beside it. Finally!

He trudged up the hill wearily. And hungrily. His jaw dropped in surprise when he saw that the cottage was made of gingerbread and resembled the gingerbread house cookies that were one of Mistress Hagscorch's specialties. He wanted to gobble the entire house right away, but there was something more important he had to do. Find Gretel!

Boldly, he knocked at the door. "Hey! Anybody home?"

He heard the thump of a cane and then the door opened. *Whoa!* He stepped back in surprise. Because framed in the doorway was a woman who was almost a dead ringer for Mistress Hagscorch, except that she had just *one* yellow eye. Her other eye was green.

"Emelda?" he guessed. "You're Mistress Hagscorch's sister, right?"

She scowled at him and replied sharply, "That's right." She stepped outside into the dusk with him and then whacked the door behind her partway closed with the tip of her cane. "Who might you be, boy? And what brings you here?" She squinted warily beyond him to the darkening forest as if expecting he'd brought bogeymen to jump out at her at any minute.

"Name's Hansel. I go to Grimm Academy and I'm looking for my sister, Gretel. Is she here?" He tried to peer around her to the inside of the cottage, but she blocked his view.

"Well, I'm afraid you've had a long trip for nothing," she told him. "She's not —"

However, before she could finish, her cane slipped from her hand. It hit the inner edge of the door behind her, causing it to open wider. "Behave, you dratted stick," Emelda muttered as she bent to pick it up.

In that moment, Hansel got a good look inside the cottage. And under a table he saw a pair of hiking boots that he knew for certain were Gretel's. He pointed to them and blurted out, "Those are my sister's boots! She's here!"

"Shh! Keep your voice down," hissed Emelda. "You'll disturb the neighbors."

"What neighbors?" asked Hansel, looking around in confusion. There were no other homes in sight.

She pointed her cane toward the Wall, which extended high in the sky. "The Barbarians and Dastardlies that live on the other side," she told him. "When they get going, they make a *terrible* racket."

Hansel peered at the Wall. Up close it looked like it was made of glass, only it was so opaque, you couldn't see through it. But just in case there really were Barbarians and Dastardlies within hearing range, he lowered his voice. "Let me in," he demanded. "I know Gretel's here."

"Yes, okay. You're right. She's here. I didn't want to say because . . . well . . . she asked me not to. She was afraid she'd get into trouble for wandering off from the Academy, and —"

Hansel frowned at her, unsure. He guessed this could be true. "Never mind all that," he told her. "Just let me see her so I know she's okay!"

Emelda sighed. "Calm down, boy. She only went downstairs to the cellar to fetch some . . . uh . . . *potatoes* for me. If you want to wait a few minutes —"

"No, I *don't* want to wait," Hansel said impatiently. "I want to see her right now!"

"If you insist." Shaking her head, the witchy-looking woman ushered him inside. After moving Gretel's boots out of the way, she quickly shoved the table aside. Then she rolled back the rug under the table and pulled up a trap-door. There was a grate under it.

"You shut the door on her while she was down there?" asked Hansel.

"What? Of course not, you suspicious boy. What a worrywart." Emelda pointed her walking stick toward the window, saying, "There's another entrance. A door to the cellar from outside. She went in that way, but I'm sure she'll come this way if you call her."

As she was opening the grate, Hansel called into the cellar. "Gretel! Are you down there?" No answer.

"It's a huge cellar and the potatoes are waaay at the back of it," said Emelda. "She just can't hear you. Step inside a ways and try again."

Hansel could see a ladder going down to the dark cellar. He started to back down it, but then stopped after just a few steps. What if this was another of Emelda's lies?

Letting go of one side of the ladder, he twisted side-ways. "Gretel! Are you down here?" he yelled into the dark abyss. Suddenly, Emelda bent toward him and gave him a shove. Losing his grip on the other side of the ladder, as well as his balance, Hansel fell. And that was the last thing he remembered.

13

Sister Act

When Gretel awoke the next morning, sun was streaming in through the little transparent-sugar window at the side of her room. It took her a few moments to remember where she was. Once she did, she jumped out of bed. She needed to get back to the Academy!

Red would be worried that she hadn't shown up at bedtime last night. Because even if Emelda had managed to get hold of Principal R through her crystal ball last night, Gretel doubted the principal would bother to tell Red where she was. Maybe her roomie would think she had slept overnight in Jill's room or something. Still, when she didn't show up for breakfast, her friends would definitely get anxious. And if they told Hansel she was missing, he'd *really* worry.

She crossed the room in her stocking feet. Just as she was about to open the bedroom door, she heard the witch talking to someone in the cottage's main room. Who else was here? she wondered. What if her dream hadn't actually been a dream and Hansel had somehow followed her to this cottage!

No, the other voice was a woman's, she realized as she listened in. "What are you up to, Emelda?" it was saying.

Gretel eased her door open a crack and peeked into the kitchen. Emelda was wearing her witch hat and was sitting at the kitchen table, partially facing the bedroom door. Before her a smallish crystal ball about the size of an orange rested on the tabletop. She was conversing with someone inside the ball, but Gretel couldn't make out the person's face. Her voice sounded familiar, though. Then it struck her. It was Mistress Hagscorch!

"You listen to me, sis," the GA cook was saying. "If that girl isn't back at the Academy by this afternoon, I'm going straight to Principal R with my suspicions."

Whoa. Mistress Scaryscorch sounds angry! And suspicions? What is that about? wondered Gretel.

"Now, Cora, I don't know what you're talking about," Emelda replied in a soothing tone. "What makes you think that girl is here anyway?"

Gretel's eyebrows shot up in surprise. Mistress Hagscorch's first name was *Cora*? And by *that girl*, did these two mean *her*?

Before she could think further, Mistress Hagscorch — *Cora*, that is — went on. "Don't you play innocent with me.

I'm your twin, remember? And I can always tell when you're lying."

Twins? No wonder Emelda was practically the spitting image of the Academy's cook except for her one green eye. Gretel had dismissed the resemblance earlier, thinking they only looked similar because they were both witchy and old. But what did Mistress Hagscorch think her sister was lying about? Was it just the fact that Gretel was here at the cottage?

Just then a sneeze came over Gretel. She tried to stifle it, but wasn't fast enough. "Ah-ah-achoo!" The force of it rocked her back onto her heels.

"Later, sis," she heard Emelda say abruptly.

Leaping lollipops! Why did she have to get sneezy just then? Gretel sprang back from the door as the thump of the woman's walking stick came toward the bedroom.

"You up at last, lazybones?" Emelda called through the door. There was a harsh edge to her voice that hadn't been there at all yesterday evening.

Gretel froze, staring at the doorknob and hoping it wouldn't turn and push the door open even wider. "Almost. Be out in a minute," she finally managed to squeak. If Mistress Hagscorch and Emelda were twin sisters, that must mean Emelda was a witch after all! Because Scaryscorch sure was. A shiver ran down her spine. However, she was beginning to sense that Mistress Hagscorch might be a *good* witch, at least compared to this one.

It struck her now that Emelda had never claimed to be a good witch. She'd only laughed when Gretel asked if she was the good or the bad kind. "*Don't be silly*," she'd replied. She'd been avoiding the question!

And suddenly, Gretel remembered the crystal ball in the Scrying classroom that Malorette and Odette had passed between them. For a brief second, she'd thought she'd seen Mistress Hagscorch's face inside that ball. Had it actually been Emelda's face, though? Could those grimm-horrible sisters have lured Gretel to that classroom just so this witch could catch a glimpse of her and listen in on what they were all saying? Had Malorette, Odette, and Emelda *planned* for Gretel to end up here? If so, why?

Deciding escape might be wise, Gretel hunted around on the floor for her boots before recalling that she'd left them under the kitchen table last night. Well, she'd just have to do without them. She ran to the transparent-sugar window and tried to lift it, but it was sealed tight. She was about to punch a fist through it so she could climb out, when the door burst open.

"What are you doing?" her host demanded.

Feigning sleepiness and yawning theatrically, Gretel said, "I wanted to get some fresh air to help me wake up. Just trying to open the window."

Emelda scowled at her. "It doesn't open. Come on, the air in the kitchen is fresher." Caught, there was nothing Gretel could do but allow the witch to take her arm and steer her firmly toward a chair at the kitchen table. The crystal ball was gone now, she noticed. And the door was firmly closed.

"Who were you talking to a little bit ago?" Gretel asked as she moved her feet around under the table, hunting for her hiking boots. They didn't seem to be in exactly the same spot she'd parked them last night.

Instead of admitting she'd been talking to her *twin sister*, Mistress Hagscorch, Emelda just shrugged. "Must have been the *wind* you heard." It was, of course, a reference to Gretel's pathetic attempt at a lie yesterday when she'd been caught eating a piece of the witch's cottage.

At last Gretel's toes touched her hiking boots. She tugged them toward herself under the table, using her feet.

Meanwhile, Emelda pulled a black cloak from a hook on the back of the kitchen door — a door that could lead to freedom if only Gretel could get through it. "I made oatsqueal for breakfast. Eat up and then come out back. I'm heating up the brick oven behind the cottage to bake bread later today and could use your help when you're ready."

"Wait. *Oven?*" Gretel's worst Hagscorch nightmare had just been rekindled. *Where was this bread Emelda planned to bake?* she wondered as she grabbed her boots and pulled them on. There was no dough rising on the kitchen counter. She supposed the witch could have made up the dough earlier that morning and taken the loaves outside already. Still, she had a very bad feeling about this!

Emelda paused, her hand on the door. Quirking an eyebrow, she looked over her shoulder at Gretel. "Is there a problem?"

"Um . . . it's just that I really need to be heading back to the Academy," she replied. "So maybe you could sketch me a map to show me the way?"

Emelda threw back her head and cackled. "All in good time, dearie." Then she picked up her walking stick from beside the door. "I'll be outside. Don't leave yet. You'll never make it without a map and I'll be happy to supply one if you'll only help me with my bread first." With a twist of the jawbreaker doorknob, she pushed through the door and outside.

Unsure what to do next, Gretel let her empty stomach decide for her. A little breakfast might help her thinking skills. At the stove, she lifted the lid from the pot of oatsqueal and spooned a large helping of the steaming porridge into the candy-cane-patterned bowl her host had left for her on the counter.

There was a small glass bottle of cinnamon mixed with sugar on the table, so after she sat down again, she sprinkled it onto the oatsqueal. *Oops!* She spilled some. As usual, she couldn't seem to eat without making at least one small mess. When she began stirring the mixture into the oatsqueal, it let out a frightful shriek that startled her so badly she dropped her spoon. With a *clink, clink, clink,* it bounced off the table and clattered to the floor.

Mistress Hagscorch's oatsqueal also made a sound when it was being stirred — but it was a shrill sound, kind of like a cross between a badly played violin and a whistle. In Gretel's imagination, the sound Emelda's oatsqueal had made was more like the scream of a torture victim!

After retrieving her spoon, Gretel washed it at the sink, and then she quickly gobbled down the oatsqueal. It wasn't nearly as tasty as Mistress Hagscorch's. Plus, it had big gray lumps in it. Clearly, Mistress Hagscorch . . . um . . . *Cora* was a better cook than her twin sister. No wonder Principal R had chosen Hagscorch over Emelda for the job at Grimm Academy.

With her stomach full now, Gretel returned to the problem of escape and finding her way back to GA. At least now she had her boots and wouldn't have to walk back in her stocking feet! Remembering what she'd overheard Mistress Hagscorch say about going straight to the principal with her suspicions if Gretel wasn't back at the Academy by that afternoon, she doubted very much that Emelda had contacted him last night as she'd promised. So maybe the first thing she should do was try to reach someone at GA herself.

Jumping up from the table, she clomped over to the kitchen cupboards and began opening one after another to search for Emelda's crystal ball. Was it possible that Hagscorch had found out about Malorette and Odette leading her into the woods and leaving her there? she wondered. Had the sisters admitted that they and Emelda had planned for Gretel to wind up at this gingerbread cottage?

She poked through a cupboard filled with baking supplies such as sugar, flour, salt, and baking powder. Finding no crystal ball, she shut that cupboard, too.

Think, think, think, she chided herself as she continued to search for the ball. If she was right that the two sisters and Emelda had plotted to bring her here, then for what purpose?

"I bet it's got something to do with E.V.I.L.," she muttered to herself.

Suddenly, she remembered about the porthole or portal or whatever, and what she'd overheard Odette say about it while hiding in the Bouquet Garden yesterday: *"And now that the butcher, the baker, and the candlestick-maker have finished building the portal* (or porthole), *it won't be long till —"*

Till what? She was stumped again.

Since she'd finished going through all the cupboards by this time, she started searching through drawers. Unless that crafty Emelda had taken it with her, the crystal ball had to be around here somewhere!

Gretel thought back to other snatches of conversation she'd overheard two days ago when she visited The Tub for candles. *"You can't tell us you didn't know what you were getting into!"* Malorette had shrieked at the butcher, the baker, and the candlestick-maker. And Odette had added that they were "well paid" for their labor. Had those little men been working for *Emelda?* Maybe they had built this gingerbread cottage. One of the men was a baker after all. But she hadn't noticed any porthole-shaped windows anywhere.

Gretel straightened and slowly looked around the tiny cottage. *If I wanted to hide a crystal ball where no one would think to look for it, where would I put it?* she asked herself.

Her eyes flicked to the icebox next to the stove. *Hmm.* She opened the icebox door and carefully surveyed the contents. A glass jar of what appeared to be eyeballs momentarily startled her, but on closer examination, they turned out to be pimiento-stuffed green olives. *Phew!* She moved the jar, a dish of butter, and a bowl of eggs aside. And finally, there behind them was the crystal ball. *Grimmtastic!*

Hurriedly, she set it on the table. Then, using a general, all-purpose spell she'd learned in Scrying class, she called up an image of her dorm room at the Academy.

"Crystal ball, give me a peek
At the vision that I seek."

Red wasn't in their room when the image of it appeared, however, so Gretel widened the view of Pearl Tower inside the ball to take in its central common area. As the image came into focus, she saw Red and her friends, Cinderella, Snow White, and Rapunzel sitting together on cushions or chairs, talking. Their voices were muffled, though, so she couldn't tell what they were talking about.

Frantically, she called out to them. Going quiet, they looked around in confusion, as if they had faintly heard her. But then, wavy lines began to run through the image in the ball, and seconds later it went dark.

"Gretel? Where are you, you lazy girl? Get out here, now!" Emelda called from somewhere outside. Gretel's heart leaped into her throat as she heard the *thump, thump,*

thump of the witch's walking stick coming toward the door. The jawbreaker doorknob rattled.

She needed to hide the crystal ball — fast! As the door began to open, she rolled it across the floor like a bowling ball, sending it straight through to the bedroom she'd slept in. It came to a stop under the bed. *Score!*

Emelda was now standing in the doorway, glaring at her. She tapped the tip of her walking stick on the floor impatiently. "Tick-tock," she said, meaning that time was passing, of course.

"Sorry. Can I just have another minute?" Gretel asked, trying to sound as apologetic as possible. "Your oatsqueal is just *sooo* delicious. Much better than the kind served at the Academy. I just can't stop eating it!" she lied. She went to the pot and began spooning a second helping into her bowl.

Emelda gave a snort, but Gretel could tell that it pleased her to think that her oatsqueal was better than her sister's. "Well, hurry up and eat. We haven't got all day," she grumbled. "There's only a small window of time before —" Her words petered out and she clamped her lips shut.

"Before what?" Gretel asked, stirring her oatsqueal. *Hmm. Window*, she thought. I bet one of the cottage windows is the portal! But even if that were true, she wasn't sure she was quite brave enough to try one of them and see where it might lead.

"Never mind," muttered the witch. She waved her stick in the air. "Just get a move on!" Then she turned away and *thump, thump, thumped* back outside.

Time to make her escape! It was now or never, thought Gretel. She ran to the bedroom and grabbed the witch's crystal ball to take with her. Once she was safely away from the cottage, she could try to use it to contact her friends again. In her haste to be away, however, she didn't get a firm hold on the ball. It slipped from her grasp as she ran into the kitchen.

"Oh, no!" she exclaimed as it fell to the floor. *Bonk!*

She expected it to break into a thousand pieces, but luckily it didn't. Instead, it just rolled onto the rug beneath the table. As she dropped to her hands and knees to crawl under the table and retrieve the ball, she heard some faint thumping noises.

For a second she went still, fearing that Emelda had returned. But then she realized that this thumping was coming from below the floorboards under the table.

And then a muffled voice from below cried out, "Gretel, is that you?"

She'd know that voice anywhere. It was Hansel's! So her dream that he was here last night hadn't been a dream after all!

14

Good Twin, Evil Twin

Gretel set the witch's crystal ball on the kitchen counter. Then she shoved the table aside and peeled back the rug. There was a wooden trapdoor under it! Quickly, she pulled it open, only to find that an iron grate covered the opening below the door. Through the grate she could see a small room below. And inside it she saw Hansel!

"Get m-m-me out of here!" he hissed, shivering with cold.

"Don't worry. I will." She rattled the grate hard, but it wouldn't give. Then she noticed the keyhole at the side of it and groaned. "It's locked!"

"So find the k-k-key," Hansel urged her, his teeth chattering.

Gretel jumped up and began to search the drawers again. Though she didn't remember seeing a key while she was looking for the crystal ball, she could have missed it since she hadn't been looking for one then.

"How did you wind up down there? The witch?" she called to her brother.

"Yeah. I didn't wake up t-t-till just a little while ago. It was last night when she tricked me into this cellar, though."

"Cellar," repeated Gretel, as she pawed through a drawer filled with odds and ends such as pebbles and twigs, bunches of dried herbs, and (shudder) *bones*! *Ick.* Why would anyone save *bones*? She hoped they came from a chicken, not a *child*! She slammed the drawer shut.

Her brother, being the dictionary wiz that he was, felt the need to define the word she'd echoed for her. "A cellar is an underground r-r-room used to store root vegetables like potatoes, carrots, and —"

"I *know* what a cellar is. I just didn't know her cottage had one," Gretel interrupted as she reached into a cupboard. She lifted out a jar filled with brightly colored balls. Its label read: SOUR CANDIES.

After giving the jar a shake and listening for the clink of a key, she pried its lid open. Instantly, the candies inside began to shout insults at her, such as "Your breath is so bad you'd make skunks run away" and "You're so dumb it would take you an hour to make minute rice." Quickly, she snapped the lid in place and shoved the jar back into the cupboard.

"Hey!" Hansel called out in a hurt voice.

"Wasn't me saying that," Gretel explained. "It was a jar of magical mean-talking candies. *Sour* ones. Probably the kind Cinderella's stepsisters eat! Ha-ha!" She made the little joke in hopes of lifting her brother's spirits, but he was apparently too tense right now to even chuckle.

On top of the counter sat a canister labeled QUICKOATS. She supposed it was what Emelda had used to make the oat-squeal. Could she have also hidden the grate key in the oats?

Gretel pulled off the lid to check, hoping the oats wouldn't start squealing or shout more insults the way the candies had. Luckily, they were quiet. But as soon as she reached down into the oats to feel around for the key, her hand became inexplicably stuck.

"When I got to the c-c-cottage last night, the witch started to c-c-claim you weren't here," Hansel piped up. Gretel heard him hopping around below in the cellar, trying to stay warm. She needed to get him out of there!

"Uh-huh," said Gretel. She tried to pull her hand out of the jar, but it only sank deeper. It seemed that these quick-oats were very much like quick*sand*!

"But then I spotted your b-b-boots under the kitchen table, so I knew she was lying," Hansel went on. "Finally, she t-t-told me you'd gone down to the cellar to fetch something for her. So she showed me this trapdoor. I was climbing d-d-down inside to find you when she gave me a push. I must've hit my head because when I woke up, you were standing up there."

"Oh," Gretel said, only half listening. She'd stopped trying to pull her hand out and was now just holding it flat with her fingers spread out. Gradually, her hand rose to the surface of the oats, and, little by little, she managed to roll it to the side of the canister and climb her fingers up the side until she could pull her hand completely free. *Phew!*

Hansel paused, then said, "Not my b-b-best idea, I guess. It was stupid of me to t-t-trust her — especially after she'd lied to me."

Hansel didn't own up to his mistakes very easily. At least not to her. The fact that he'd admitted he'd made one now softened her heart toward him.

"We all make mistakes." It hadn't been her best idea to go into the woods with Malorette and Odette either. "How did you find me here?" she asked him as she dragged a chair over and stood on it to check the tops of the cupboards.

"After you left the Great Hall, I watched through a window to see where you went, and I saw you go off with Malorette and Odette." He sighed.

At this, she almost fell off her chair. So he knew what she'd done! *Argh!*

"I was worried, and I really w-w-wanted to follow you, but I d-d-didn't."

"Why not?" Gretel asked in surprise.

Hansel sighed again. "I was trying to give you some space and not ch-ch-check up on you. I know you think I'm . . . well . . . *bossy* . . . sometimes."

"I never said that," Gretel protested, even though she'd *thought* it often enough. Hopping off the chair, she dragged it back to the table. The cupboards had turned out to be covered with a thick layer of dust. But no key.

"Anyway, I kept an eye out for your r-r-return," Hansel continued. "When I saw Malorette and Odette come into the Great Hall near the end of lunch, Jack and I got in the lunch line behind them. And then Jack spotted a red ribbon sticking out of Odette's pocket that he recognized as yours. Turned out she had a whole pocketful of your ribbons! You should've seen Jack b-b-blush when I asked him later what kind of guy notices a girl's hair ribbons."

Jack had noticed the ribbons she wore in her hair? Of course she also used them as trail markers. Maybe that's why he'd recognized them. A warm feeling washed over Gretel at this information, but she didn't have time to mull it over. She needed to find that key!

She checked a new drawer. Nope. While withdrawing her hand, she accidentally flipped over a piece of paper and saw it was a drawing of two young girls about her own age. They were twins, except that one had two yellow eyes and the other had a yellow eye and a green eye. Cora and Emelda!

"Hey, what's going on!" Hansel called since she hadn't spoken for a while. "Are you still there?"

"Yes! Still key searching," she called back. She set the drawing on top of the counter next to the crystal ball and continued checking drawers. "So what happened then?"

"M-M-Malorette and Odette said how they'd played a little trick on you. Leaving you alone in N-N-Neverwood Forest and taking all the ribbons you'd tied to m-m-mark your trail."

"Some trick," Gretel grumped. She peeked out the window. No sign of the witch coming back so far, but she was running out of time.

"That's exactly what J-J-Jack said," Hansel told her. "And that's when Mistress Hagscorch jumped into the conversation. She said she'd talked to her sister, Emelda, by crystal ball the night before. And that Emelda had told her Malorette and Odette were in cahoots on some plan that — if it worked — would alter the c-c-course of Grimmlandia history and 'advance Emelda's status in E.V.I.L.'"

"Whoa!" Obviously, Gretel had been right to worry that the Society was still operating despite recent setbacks. "What was the plan?"

"Jack and I couldn't get anything else out of Malorette

and Odette. But then Hagscorch started d-d-doing her scary act, you know, calling them dearies and pinching their cheeks and saying how tasty they looked?"

"Yeah, I know," said Gretel. Only too well!

"Well, then those girls finally started talking!" said Hansel. "They said the plan has something to do with freeing Ms. Wicked from the Dark Nothingterror. Not only that, they handed over a map they had of how to get to the cottage so we could use it to come here."

"We?" echoed Gretel from across the room. She noticed that Hansel seemed to have stopped shivering. She could hear him hopping up and down. Thankfully, the activity must be helping to warm him up. She went back to searching for the key, this time in some spice jars.

"Jack and me," Hansel answered. "He was coming with me to find you. Only, when we were leaving the Academy, he stumbled on the drawbridge and twisted his ankle. So I had to leave him behind."

Since Hansel couldn't see her from where he was, Gretel did a quick little happy dance in spite of the danger they were in. Because it was so sweet that Jack had been willing to brave danger to help find her!

"Anyway," Hansel continued, "Malorette and Odette finally admitted to us that they *did* know Hagscorch's sister, and —"

"Her *twin* sister," Gretel put in. "And Mistress Hagscorch's name is Cora." She grabbed the drawing from the counter and slid the sketch through the bars of the grate so Hansel could see it. "That's them as kids. Except for the eyes, they look the same."

Hansel nodded. "Only Hagscorch is the good twin and her sister is the evil twin."

"Guess so," Gretel agreed. "I've always been scared of Hagscorch because she's so witchy. But now I've decided that, despite her weirdness, she means no harm."

"I bet Emelda does, though," Hansel handed her back the drawing, pushing it through the grate. "Do you think she took the key with her?"

"I'll keep looking, but I'm beginning to think she did," Gretel said, shoving the drawing into her pocket. She was starting to feel frantic. What if Emelda returned to the cottage to find out why it was taking her so long to come outside? If she saw that Gretel had found her brother, there would be trouble.

Before she could discuss this with Hansel, he said, "Another thing. Odette said Emelda ordered them to bring a student into the forest, but only about halfway to the cottage."

"Maybe she just didn't want them at her house?" Gretel speculated.

"Maybe. Anyway, I feel to blame that they chose you. See, when Jack and I were leaving the infirmary on Friday, we ran into the two of them. And after Jack told them we were planning to go hiking, they asked me if I was a good hiker."

"So?" said Gretel.

"So I boasted that you and I have been hiking trails since we were old enough to walk," Hansel explained, sounding miserable. "That's why they picked you!"

Gretel shook her head. "Don't blame yourself. I'm the one who agreed to go with them." She thought about telling him how Malorette and Odette had tricked her with their talk about finding Mr. Hump-Dumpty's (nonexistent) secret place, but then decided that could wait till later.

"Those . . ." Gretel searched for the right word to describe girls who'd form such evil plans. Nothing seemed horrible enough, so she settled on ". . . brats!" Then she remembered how great her brother was with words, and asked him, "Hey, Hansel, what exactly is a portal? I know it's like an opening or a window or door. But what's it usually for?"

Without hesitation, he told her, "A portal *can* be a magical doorway that allows someone to cross over from one magical land to another. Why are you asking?"

Gretel gasped and ran over to stare down at him again. "Because I heard those grimmawful sisters say something about a portal," she said, leaving out for now that the men from The Tub had apparently built it and that at first she'd thought it was a port*hole* they'd constructed. "But they never said where this portal was. Or who it was meant to transport."

For a few seconds they stared at each other through the grate. Then, at the same time they both said, "Ms. Wicked!"

Thump! Thump! Hearing the sudden dreaded sound, Gretel whipped her eyes toward the door. "Shh! The witch is coming!" she hissed at Hansel. "I'm going to close you back in."

"What? Wait!" Hansel tried to argue.

"No! If Emelda finds out I know you're here, she'll make sure we can't ever get that key. So keep quiet for now. I promise I'll help you escape."

Just in time, she shut the trapdoor, flipped the rug over it, and slid the table back into its usual spot. At the very last moment, she remembered the crystal ball, still on top of the counter. She grabbed it and shoved it into the nearest drawer. Then she picked up her empty oatmeal bowl from the table and deliberately dashed it against the floor so that it smashed to pieces. *Crash!*

15

The Great Bake-Off

Gretel grabbed a broom and was sweeping up the pieces of her broken bowl when the witch pushed in through the door.

"Clumsy girl!" Emelda scolded, looking at the mess. "So this is what's been taking you so long!"

"I'm really sorry," Gretel apologized. She dumped the broken pieces into the trash. "I went to wash the bowl and it slipped."

Luckily, her trick to explain her delay in getting outside had worked. The witch didn't seem to suspect anything. Truthfully, Gretel wasn't at all sorry to have broken the bowl. In fact, she would've liked to smash a few more of Emelda's dishes! And then push Emelda into that cellar and see how she liked it. Only first she had to get Hansel out.

She watched the witch's eyes stray to the rug covering the trapdoor. A wicked smile came over her wrinkled face. Was she thinking about Hansel being not far away?

Thinking it was her private little joke that he was down below in the cellar? Pulling a key from her pocket, she casually placed it on the table. She probably got a kick out of acting so cruelly, thinking that Gretel would have no idea what the key was for.

Gretel's heart beat faster. *Did* it in fact open the trapdoor grate? She considered making a lunge for the key to find out, but held back for now. Best to think and act carefully. The witch might be old, but she didn't exactly look frail. She seemed to walk just fine without the use of her walking stick when she wanted to. And who knew how powerful her magic might be?

"Come," Emelda ordered Gretel. She pointed her stick at the door. "You promised to help me with the bread."

"You go on," Gretel replied, trying not to look at the key. "I'll clean the oatsqueal pot on the stove first and then come out, okay? I hate to leave your cute kitchen a mess." As soon as the witch was out of sight, she planned to grab the key, unlock the grate, and release Hansel so they could both escape.

"Leave the pot," the witch said testily. "Come outside. Now!" She thumped her walking stick on the floor for emphasis.

Reluctantly, Gretel left the cottage ahead of the witch. "Since when is baking bread a two-person job?" she asked.

"Go around to the backyard. I'll explain there," Emelda ordered, avoiding her question for now. "We don't have much time."

"Why the big hurry?" Gretel asked.

"The timing for these things must be just right," the witch replied craftily.

When Gretel saw the big brick oven at the back of the cottage, she stopped and gasped. It jutted out from the frosted glass Wall as if built right into it!

Emelda nudged her forward again. As Gretel's gaze roved over the oven, it suddenly struck her that it must be brand-new. The bricks were exceptionally clean — completely soot-free. As if the oven had just been built and never been used. It was well crafted, though, with small pieces of brick set in a decorative mosaic pattern high above its front opening.

Remembering that she'd seen no bread dough rising on the kitchen counter, Gretel glanced around. There were no bowls or loaves of dough out here, either. There wasn't even a table to set stuff on. Now she was even more certain that the witch was lying about her bread-baking project. But why?

When they reached the oven, Emelda gestured a wrinkled hand toward it. "Hop up and climb inside," she instructed Gretel.

"What? Why?" asked Gretel, backing a few steps away from the oven instead. "That seems a little dangerous." Warmed by burning wood, brick ovens heated slowly. However, once the brick walls absorbed the heat, the temperature inside could get *really* hot.

Emelda smiled in a way she probably thought was comforting, but Gretel could tell it wasn't a genuine smile. "Don't worry. I just need you to see if the port, er, oven has gotten warm enough for baking yet. And that's the best way to check the temperature."

Huh? Maybe she should give this witch a nickname like the ones she'd given Hagscorch, thought Gretel. She knew just the one that would fit. Mistress Childmuncher! Because it sounded like Emelda was planning to bake Gretel for lunch in this oven. And then she'd probably roast Hansel later for dinner!

Her eyes slid sideways toward the cottage. Could she make it there, get the key from the table, and release Hansel before this witch caught up? Maybe if she was very lucky, but would they have time to make their escape into the forest, too? Probably not.

Gretel shuddered, trying to think of another plan. "But how am I supposed to get up that high? Do you have a ladder or some steps?" she whined, stalling for time.

The witch let out a frustrated huff. "Here, I'll give you a boost," she suggested, stepping forward.

With little choice, Gretel sidled closer to the oven. "Oh! Wait. My boot's untied," she announced. Going down on one knee beside the oven, she pretended to retie the already-tied boot.

But she'd noticed something really weird as she'd stepped closer to the oven. The wood in the bottom part of it hadn't even been lit. So no heat was coming from it. Which meant Emelda probably wasn't planning to cook Gretel for lunch after all!

Well, that was a relief. Sort of. But she still didn't want to climb inside the oven. It was a sure thing that the witch was up to something. And whatever it was was not likely to be to Gretel's benefit!

As she was pondering this, the significance of the slip the witch had made, while asking her to check to see if the oven was warm, suddenly dawned on her. *Port,* Emelda had said by mistake. She'd goofed and almost said *portal* instead of *oven*, only Gretel had been too scared and worried to figure that out till now.

"Hurry up! How long does it take to tie a boot?" Emelda asked crabbily.

"Just a second longer. My other boot came untied, too,"

said Gretel. She didn't look up for fear that the witch would read in her eyes what Gretel had guessed.

Because suddenly, all the snippets of things Gretel had overheard or been told in the last two days had snapped into place like puzzle pieces. This oven was the very portal that the butcher, the baker, and the candlestick-maker had made! She was sure of it! But that still didn't explain why Emelda wanted her to go inside it.

Her mind raced to figure out the answer. Hansel had said that portals could be magical doorways that allowed one to cross over from one magical land to another. This must be how the E.V.I.L. Society intended to bring Ms. Wicked back from the Nothingterror and into Grimmlandia. It was also how Emelda hoped to alter Grimmlandia history and "advance her status" in the society. But why did they need Gretel?

"Time's up," said the witch, taking Gretel's arm and nudging her toward the oven.

Noooo! Gretel fought back the fear rising within her. She was sure some kind of doom was close at hand. *I am not afraid. I am not afraid,* she repeated over and over in her head. Even as she dragged her heels, she tried to act casual and pretend she didn't know what was really going on.

While the oven loomed, Gretel took note of something she hadn't bothered to study earlier. Those small pieces of brick set in a mosaic pattern above the oven's opening. They spelled these words: THE GIVE AND TAKE AND BAKE OVEN.

The answer to why Emelda and the Society needed her came in a flash. *She* — or someone like her — must be required to make the oven's magic work! One person had to be *given* in exchange for the *taking* of another. And she was meant to switch places with Ms. Wicked! To be the person sent to replace that teacher in the Dark Nothingterror!

"Sorry, I can't d-d-do it," she began as she peered into the oven. Try as she might, she couldn't keep her voice from trembling. "The opening is too small."

"Bah!" exclaimed the witch. "You'll fit in there easy. Stand aside and I'll show you."

"Oh, thank you!" Gretel replied. "That would be perfect."

The witch leaned her walking stick up against the oven. Then she stuck her head inside the opening. "See? It's plenty big enough. I could get in myself."

"Then let me help you!" Gretel exclaimed. With all her strength, she gave the witch a mighty shove. Emelda tumbled through the opening! At the exact same moment, Gretel saw Ms. Wicked's face push through the Wall at the back of the oven portal.

For a split second, Gretel worried that E.V.I.L.'s plan would work, and that Ms. Wicked would be returned to Grimmlandia. But then, for some reason, Ms. Wicked and Emelda were both sucked, howling, through the back of the oven!

16

Help!

Feeling both jubilant and rattled at the sudden disappearance of Ms. Wicked and the witch, Gretel spun around and hurried over to the gingerbread cottage.

"I'm back!" she called as she ran inside, hoping Hansel would hear and be reassured. After grabbing the key, she shoved the table aside, peeled back the rug, and pulled up the trapdoor. As she unlocked the grate and freed her brother, she quickly explained what had just happened with The Give and Take and Bake Oven portal.

"I don't get it," he said as he climbed out. "Why wasn't Ms. Wicked returned to Grimmlandia through the portal to take Emelda's place?"

"I don't know. Who cares?" said Gretel. "Maybe it required a young person like me to go through. Or maybe you have to exchange good for evil. Only both of those ladies were evil, so the magic didn't work right. Those are my theories any — Hey," she interrupted herself. "You have my backpack! Odette offered to carry it for a while yesterday, but then she and Malorette tricked me and ran off."

"Yeah, that sounds like them." Shrugging the backpack off, Hansel handed it to her. "I found it on the trail. They'd emptied it out and left it there."

"Oh, no! My pocketknife was in it!"

"If they've l-l-lost it, I'll get you a n-n-new one," Hansel promised, beginning to shiver again.

Quickly, Gretel ran and grabbed the puffy pink comforter from the bed she'd slept in last night and wrapped it around him. While he huddled in it, trying to get warm again, she opened the drawer where she'd stashed the witch's crystal ball and took it out.

Hansel jerked his chin to indicate the ball. "What's that for?"

"We should try to contact someone at the Academy to let them know we're okay," she explained. After placing the ball in her backpack, she slung the pack's straps over her shoulder. "Later, though. Let's get out of here while we can. This cottage may look sweet and cute, but it gives me the creeps."

When they got outside, Hansel screeched to a halt. "Wait! I'm starving. All I had to eat last night was raw vegetables in that cellar. And I want to see the portal before we go. Just to make sure no one came through." He broke off a roof tile just as Gretel had the day before and began nib-bling it.

"No, let's leave!" argued Gretel.

Since Hansel wouldn't listen, all she could do was fol-low him around to the back of the cottage. Then, while he munched the tile and studied the oven thoroughly, she explained that it had been built by the butcher, the baker, and the candlestick-maker.

"I knew those Rub-A-Dub-Dub guys couldn't be trusted," Hansel exclaimed. "They really are knaves. But they do know how to build an oven. This thing is awesome!"

Gretel rolled her eyes. "I don't care how well built it is, it gives me the creeps just as much as that cottage!" She thought back to what Malorette and Odette had said to the men in The Tub. About how the men knew what they were getting into and were well paid for their work and silence.

Maybe they *had* known they were building a portal, but she'd bet anything they hadn't understood what Emelda intended to use it for. In any case it had sounded as if they later regretted their part in the scheme. "I'm not so sure those guys totally understood what Emelda and E.V.I.L. intended to do with the portal till it was too late," she told Hansel.

"Well, if you're right, then they should have told Principal R about the whole portal project as soon as they *did* suspect the group was up to no good." Hansel climbed up on the oven and poked his head in.

"Get down from there!" Gretel exclaimed. "It's probably still working. For all we know, it might suck you into the Nothingterror, too!"

"I'm just trying to . . ." Hansel began.

But Gretel didn't hear the rest because her eyes fell on the walking stick. It was still leaning up against the brick oven where the witch had left it. But when Hansel continued to examine the oven's opening, the stick took a couple of thumping steps toward Gretel. Then it flew into her hand.

"Yikes! Get away from me, you awful thing!" she yelled at it. She shook her hand free and the stick spun dizzily in the air before falling to the grass a dozen feet away.

"Run!" she called to Hansel. "That's Emelda's evil walking stick. It found me and led me to her cottage yesterday!" She didn't add that the reason she'd been so willing to follow the stick was because she'd thought it must be her (non-evil) magical charm.

Finally, her brother listened to her. He leaped down from the oven and the two of them took off down the hill.

Thump! Thump! "That horrible stick is following us!" yelled Gretel. "Leave us alone!" she shouted back at the stick.

But no matter what she yelled at it or how fast they moved, they could still hear the stick thumping behind them. They didn't stop running until they reached the bottom of the hill and entered Neverwood Forest.

Still breathing hard from her run, Gretel cupped a hand around her ear to listen. "I don't hear the thumps anymore," she said after a while.

"Good." Hansel pulled Malorette and Odette's trail map from his pocket. After consulting it, he pointed to where the trail split up ahead. "We go right," he told her.

They'd only just taken the fork to the right, however, when they saw the stick standing in the middle of the path ahead of them.

"What do we do now?" Hansel whispered to her. "We have to go that way."

"Follow me. And let's stick together," said Gretel. "Er, *stay* together."

With her in the lead, they moved carefully toward the witch's stick, intending to pass it. Gretel breathed a sigh of relief when she made it past with no trouble. But where was Hansel? She gasped when she looked back to see he had halted next to the stick and was examining it closely.

"What are you doing?" she demanded.

"Our grandfather used to make walking sticks like this one," he commented.

"Yes, I remember," said Gretel. "He sold them in his shop along with the other things he carved. He promised to make something special for me when I was older, but . . ." her voice trailed off as a wave of sadness washed over her without warning.

"No, I mean, I think he actually made this one," Hansel clarified. He waved her closer and then pointed to a tiny carving of a duck down near the base of the walking stick.

Gretel bent down to look. She rubbed the pad of her fingertip across the duck as Hansel held the stick. "That's Grandfather's trademark!" she said in wonder. "He carved it on every item he made."

"I know!" said Hansel. "So what happened? Did that witch buy it from his shop and then turn it evil?"

Gretel straightened up, frowning. "Or maybe she stole it. I wouldn't put it past her."

Hansel rotated the stick in his hands and squinted at something on it. "There are some tiny letters here under one of the knots, did you notice?"

"Nuh-uh," said Gretel. Now that she knew their grandfather had made the stick, she kind of wished she could hang on to it as a keepsake. Too bad Emelda had made it evil!

"F O R G R — I can't quite make out the last four letters."

"Let me see." Gretel started to reach toward the stick, but just then Hansel's stomach growled. "You've hardly eaten a thing today, have you? Just that one thin roof tile," she said sympathetically.

Remembering how the walking stick had seemed to grant her rhymed request once before (unless it truly had just been heading for home), she tried again. "Hey, stick. We need something to eat — and make it sweet."

Suddenly, the stick took off. *Thump. Thump. Thump.* It blazed a new trail straight through the underbrush, wide enough for them to follow single file.

"Wait for us!" Gretel ran after it and so did Hansel. Unfortunately, they soon wound up at the cottage again.

"You dumb stick!" yelled Gretel. "You led us right back to this same grimmcreepy place!" The stick looked a little droopy at her scolding.

But as Hansel reached up to a window shutter and broke off a piece of gingerbread cookie, Gretel remembered that she *had* asked the stick to find them something sweet.

"Mmm, good," Hansel murmured as he crammed the cookie into his mouth and chewed.

Gretel looked at the stick in apology. "Sorry, I guess you were only following my orders." Without warning, the walking stick leaped into her hands. *Yikes!* She started to throw it away again, but then under her fingertips she felt the carved letters Hansel had discovered. She turned the stick till she could squint at them.

"F O R G R . . . Hey, wait, there's a bigger space between the first *R* and the *G*. I think it's two words," she told Hansel.

He cocked his head, and spoke between bites. "FOR GR? What's that mean?"

She squinted harder until she could make out the last four letters. "The other letters are *ETEL*?"

Hansel straightened and chewed really fast as if he had something important to announce. He swallowed and then at the same time, the answer burst from them both. "FOR GRETEL!"

Gretel looked from the stick to her brother. "Grandfather must've meant this walking stick to be mine! When I was lost and it led me through Neverwood Forest, I thought it might be my magical charm," she confessed to him now. "But it can't be, can it? Because magical charms only do what the person they belong to tells them to do, and this stick was obeying Emelda."

Hansel wiped a smear of pink frosting from his chin with the back of one hand, then licked it off his knuckles. "She must've put a spell on it. To make it think it *did* belong to her — for a time. But Grandfather made it for you, so I bet that any spell that witch put on it was broken when she was sucked into the Nothingterror."

"Do you think so?" Gretel asked wistfully. At her question, the stick leaped from her arms. In a patch of dirt near the cottage, it drew a big heart. Then it returned to her hand, snuggling into it.

Hansel grinned. "I think it's saying, 'I'm Yours.' Or maybe 'Be Mine.' Sort of a stick valentine."

Flap! Flap! Just then, a flock of geese appeared overhead. The kind that carried things from here to there in the Academy's Grimmstone Library. In groups of three these geese were pulling fancy chariots, hitched by long ribbons to each of the vehicles.

When the geese flew in for a landing, Gretel could see GA students seated inside the chariots. There was Jack and Jill! And Red! And also the butcher, baker, candlestick-maker, and Hagscorch, too! Everyone was out looking for her and her brother!

First out of the chariots was Jill, who raced to hug Gretel. "I'm so glad you're okay!" she cried. When she stepped back, she added, "And I love your haircut. Cute!"

The instant she let go, Red wrapped Gretel in another hug. "I was so worried about you! And ditto on the hair."

Some of the other girls came to hug her and admire her new hairstyle, too. Including Snow White, who added, "Ms. Goose let us borrow the library geese so we could come to your rescue. It was Principal R's idea to bring the chariots. He would have come with us. Only, not knowing how E.V.I.L. planned to use the portal, he decided to stay at GA in case the Society was plotting an attack on the Academy."

"You know about the portal?" Gretel said in surprise, glancing around the group.

Everyone nodded. As more GA students gathered near, Mistress Hagscorch came over and pinched her cheek. "You little dearie! It's good to see you're okay!" Over the cook's shoulder, Gretel saw Jack talking to Hansel a distance away. When their eyes caught, Jack flashed her a heart-meltingly dimpled smile and sent her a thumbs-up.

Before she could smile back at him, the cook drew her attention again. "After Hansel left with the map to find you, I was in such a stew I hardly slept last night! Right after breakfast this morning, I took the whole problem of my sister to Principal R. And here we are."

Mistress Hagscorch paused to gaze toward the cottage. "I'd heard that Emelda had copied my gingerbread cookie recipe to make a life-size house to live in. Is she in there?"

Gulp! Gretel knew she'd have to break the bad news about Emelda being sucked into the Dark Nothingterror, but before she could say anything about it, Jack and Hansel came over. Somehow, Jack managed to pick up right where

Hagscorch's story had left off. "This morning, Principal R called everyone who might know anything into his office," he told Gretel. "Together we all tried to figure out what Mistress Hagscorch's sister and E.V.I.L. could be planning."

"My stepsisters are in deep doo-doo for their part in all this," Cinderella noted gaily. "They've been suspended from the Academy 'until further notice'."

Rapunzel punched a fist in the air. "Yeah! It's about time!" Other students giggled at this.

Gretel grinned, too, glad of the news. Those two had been trouble with a capital *T* at GA for a very long time. And now she might never have to see them again!

As the others talked, Mistress Hagscorch started toward the cottage.

"Wait! We have to tell you something," Gretel called out.

Mistress Hagscorch turned back. Before anyone else could speak, Gretel and Hansel rushed to tell their story. The cook gasped when she learned that her sister had locked Hansel in the cottage cellar and had tried to send Gretel to the Dark Nothingterror in order to bring Ms. Wicked back to Grimmlandia. Although appalled at her sister's actions, she turned quite pale when she learned that Emelda was now lost to the Nothingterror herself.

"If we'd known what she was up to, we never would've taken her dough to do the job," said the baker.

"We've seen the light now, though," said the candlestick-maker. "And we're here to make things right."

"Come on, then," the butcher said to the other two men. "We've got our work cut out for us." Off they went, with tools they'd brought with them, to tear down the brick oven.

Determined to help, everyone else followed. Together, they hauled away the bricks the workmen tore down. Using sledgehammers, they reduced the bricks to rubble so there'd be no chance they could ever be used to build a portal again.

When Gretel found herself kneeling in the grass and wielding a hammer next to Mistress Hagscorch, she paused to give her the drawing she'd found in the cottage kitchen.

Mistress Hagscorch's yellow eyes lit up as she grasped it in her clawed hands. "Thank you," she said. "I can't believe Emelda saved this after all these years. We never got along well. Not since we were this age, at any rate. And after Principal R hired me instead of her to cook for the Academy, things between us grew even worse. I fear that may be one reason she got involved with E.V.I.L. — to try to make her mark some other way."

She pushed a lock of her straggly white-gray hair behind one ear. "Still," she said with a sigh. "For better or worse, she was . . . *is* . . . my sister."

Gretel thought she understood how you could care deeply about someone close to you without liking or approving of their behavior. But though Hansel might occasionally say or do something that annoyed her, at least he was *not* evil. Far from it, in fact!

Mistress Hagscorch gazed toward the Wall. "The Nothingterror is a better place for her, really. She can make all the evil plans she wants to there, but Grimmlandia will be safe because she won't be here to carry them out. Besides, she'll have Ms. Wicked for company. They should get along just fine since they're so much alike. Birds of a feather, as the saying goes."

Any remaining doubts Gretel might have had about Hagscorch being a *good* witch had completely evaporated by now. And her former fear of the cook was replaced by feelings of sympathy. "Even if your sister and Ms. Wicked become friends, I bet she'll still miss you," she said.

Mistress Hagscorch nodded. "We kept in contact with weekly crystal ball visits." Her voice broke a little and a tear rolled down her cheek as she added, "Despite our disagreements, I'll miss talking to her."

Gretel wished she could help. Suddenly, she remembered that she had Emelda's crystal ball. After slipping her bright-blue backpack from her shoulders, she unzipped it and reached inside. Then she handed the ball to Mistress Hagscorch.

"My sister's?" she asked in delight.

Hansel came over just then. Gretel nodded. "Maybe you can send it to her so you two will still be able to talk once in a while. I heard that Principal R was able to launch that trouble-making sprite Jack Frost over the Wall inside a glass snow globe."

An evil mastermind, the sprite she'd spoken of had recently plotted to use Snowflake's magical ice and snow-making abilities to rule Grimmlandia. When he hadn't succeeded, he'd asked Principal R to send him to a place where he could realize his dream of becoming an evil pup-pet master. Principal R hadn't hesitated to oblige!

"So sending your sister a crystal ball should be a piece of cake," Hansel agreed.

"Snowflake and Rapunzel have gotten pretty good with their catapulting lately. They'll help, I'm sure," Gretel added.

Hansel's forehead wrinkled in thought. "But wouldn't your sister or Ms. Wicked or other members of E.V.I.L. be able to use the ball to communicate with their E.V.I.L. coun-terparts in Grimmlandia?"

"Oh!" said Gretel. "I hadn't thought about that!"

The cook had begun polishing the ball with the edge of her apron. "Luckily," she told them with a smile, "I know a lockdown spell that would make it so my sister, or anyone else using her ball, would only be able to contact me."

Gretel smiled. "Problem solved."

"Last brick!" yelled Jack from across the yard. He brought down a hammer on it, smashing it to bits. Everyone cheered.

Now that the oven was completely dismantled and the bricks all pounded to rubble, Mistress Hagscorch stood and stretched. "I bet you've all worked up an appetite, haven't you?" she called out to the dozen or so students who had made the trip to the cottage.

A chorus of "*Yeah*" greeted her question. With a touch of her wicked humor, she added, "And from the look of you all, I'd say you could use a little fattening up."

Laughter erupted at this familiar phrase. For once, Gretel giggled along with everyone else. And just like that, the last of her fears about the cook fell away.

"So what are you all waiting for?" Mistress Hagscorch said. She pointed at the gingerbread cottage. "Go. Eat. My sister built it using my recipe, so it's the one thing around here that's tasty!"

No one needed a second invitation. The students descended on the cottage like a swarm of locusts and had a great deal of fun eating it to the ground. The furnishings, tableware, and other things that remained were loaded into chariots.

"These are artifacts that must be stored in the Grimmstone Library," Mistress Hagscorch noted. "Whatever crumbs remain behind can be left for hungry critters and time to destroy."

17

Happy Trails

There wasn't room for the students in the loaded chariots, so only the three workmen from The Tub and Mistress Hagscorch rode on them back to the Academy. "See you at dinnertime," the cook called back to the students as the geese lifted off.

The students groaned. And Gretel knew why! Having eaten their fill of the cottage, she doubted any of them (including herself) would want dinner that night, despite the deliciousness of Mistress Hagscorch's cooking.

"I hope we don't get lost on our way back," Red said anxiously as the group of students headed into the forest on foot. With her poor sense of direction, she'd gotten lost many a time, even around the Academy.

"Don't worry," Gretel told her. "Hansel's got a map." Then, with a grin, she brandished her walking stick. "And my magical charm is good at blazing trails!"

Exclamations of *"What?" "Your magical charm?"* and *"When?"* rang out.

As the students hiked through the forest with Hansel in the lead, Gretel told everyone about her walking stick and how it had once belonged to the witch but was intended for her, made by her grandfather.

Naturally, her friends were all excited for her. "Show us what it can do!" Jill urged. Before Gretel could reply, a vine snaked down from a tree they were walking under and wrapped itself around her BFF's arm. Jill tried to shake off the vine, but to no avail.

"Stick of mine, please make that vine stay in line," Gretel said quickly. Her stick leaped from her hand to obey. One good whack was enough to make the vine loosen its hold on Jill's arm and wiggle away.

"Grimmawesome!" Jill exclaimed as the stick flew back to Gretel and settled under her hand again.

"It can also flatten down grasses to create new trails," she told her friends. "And help find food and water! Not sure what else it can do yet." She didn't tell them that when she'd first held it, she felt braver. And that it made her feel braver now, too. She had a feeling that was part of why this charm was meant for her. But she wanted more time to explore all that before sharing those thoughts with others.

Hansel overheard her as he stopped to consult his map. "Create new trails, huh?"

"Yeah, I was thinking I could write a supplement to *A Guide to Trails and Hikes Around Grimmlandia*! And include the new trails it makes as well as others I discover," Gretel blurted out. She hadn't meant to let the cat out of the bag so soon, and braced herself for her brother's criticism.

But instead of pointing out holes in her plan, as she'd halfway expected him to do, he called back to her in an admiring tone, "That's a grimmerrific idea! Let me know if you need help!"

"Thanks," she said, as he directed everyone toward the left fork of the trail they'd been hiking along. With his love of words and dictionaries, he'd be an extra big help with one thing in particular. "I'll take you up on that offer, especially when it comes to naming the trails," she called back.

Hansel grinned at her. "Perfect. Right up my alley!"

Jack had been hiking beside Hansel at the head of the group, but now he dropped back to the rear with Gretel, Jill, and Red. "I'll help with your trail guide, too," he told Gretel. "I bet lots of kids will."

"Count me in," said his sister, Jill.

Gretel flushed with pleasure. "That would be great, you guys." Then a new idea came to her. "Maybe members of

G.O.O.D. could band together to improve old trails in addition to creating new ones."

"G.O.O.D. idea," said Jack. He spoke each letter in turn, which made everyone who heard laugh.

"We could put up signs to warn hikers of dangerous areas," Jill said enthusiastically.

"Yeah," said Red. "Like the Wall. I could maybe borrow some of the Drama department's supplies to help us make the signs."

"There are other improvements we could make, too. Like building bridges over mushy areas, and removing fallen tree limbs or vines that block some trails now," said Hansel, dropping back to walk with them as well.

Jack grinned at him. "I like it. Less for me to trip over!"

The girls all laughed.

A bit farther up the trail, Gretel stopped for a moment to empty out a pebble that had worked its way into her boot. She waved the others on ahead, saying, "Go on. I'll catch up."

When Jack stayed behind, she passed him her walking stick to hold while she turned her boot upside down to shake out the pebble. As she started to teeter while standing on one foot, Jack took her arm to steady her.

"Thanks," she said, feeling her cheeks warm. She'd noticed earlier that his forehead injury must have healed because the bandage was gone now. However, he was limping slightly, probably from his stumble on the drawbridge that Hansel had mentioned. "How's your ankle?" she asked as she slipped her boot back on.

"Not too bad," he told her. When she straightened at last, he held her walking stick out to her.

"You keep it for now," she told him. "It'll help take the weight off that ankle."

"Thanks," he said. "I've got something for you, too. Here. A gift from the abominable sisters." He pulled out a bunch of ribbons from his pocket and handed them to her.

Gretel laughed. "Thanks, these'll come in handy marking the new trails," she said, stuffing her ribbons in her pocket.

They had just begun to walk again when a loud howl came from directly behind them. *Owooooo!*

Startled, Gretel grabbed Jack's free hand. *Was it a wolf?*

As the two of them jumped around to see what was behind them, laughter rang out.

"Got you, didn't I?" A boy stepped out from behind a tree. It was only Red's crush, Wolfgang, playing a practical joke.

Jack grinned at him. "I'll get you for that," he said good-naturedly. "Sometime when you least expect it."

Wolfgang grinned back. "Ha! You're on." With that, he loped past them and called over his shoulder, "See you back at GA!"

Realizing she was still holding Jack's hand, Gretel started to drop it as they began to walk again. But then she thought better of it and left her hand in his. And he didn't let go!

A grimmtastically happy feeling filled her. What an incredible adventure she'd had! Yes, parts of it had been very scary, but she'd survived and even kept her wits about her, especially at the end.

And she'd gotten a magic charm! It was even more special because her grandfather had carved it for her. She could hardly wait to use it to help G.O.O.D. with trail projects.

She had a new appreciation for Hansel now, too. It seemed he was going to try not to be so bossy from here on out, and she would try to cut him a little more slack when he was. Plus, she'd finally come to see Mistress Hagscorch as the *good* witch she'd always been. And then there was Jack . . .

She was holding the hand of a boy she liked for the very first time! So her super-secret crush on him probably wasn't going to be super secret much longer. But that was fine with her. Gretel smiled over at him and he smiled back. Swinging their hands between them, they raced (or race-limped in Jack's case) down the trail to catch up with their friends.

A Grimmtastic girl named Cinderella is starting her first week at Grimm Academy on the wrong foot. Cinda's totally evil stepsisters are out to make her life miserable. The Steps tease Cinda, give her terrible advice about life at the Academy, and even make her look bad in front of her new friends, Red, Snow, and Rapunzel! But when Cinda overhears the Steps plotting a villainous deed that could ruin Prince Awesome's ball, Cinda, her new friends, and a pair of magical glass slippers have to stop them — before the last stroke of midnight!

Red Riding Hood is thrilled to try out for the school play. Acting is her dream, and she's great at it — too bad she has stage fright! After a grimmiserable audition, Red decides to focus on helping her friends Cinda, Snow, and Rapunzel save Grimm Academy from the E.V.I.L. Society. But when Red gets lost in Neverwood Forest and runs into Wolfgang, who might be part of E.V.I.L., she needs her magic basket and a grimmazingly dramatic performance to figure out what's going on!

No matter how many lucky charms she wears, Snow White can't catch a break. She's especially worried that her step-mom, Ms. Wicked, is a member of the E.V.I.L. Society. Snow and her friends Red, Cinda, and Rapunzel are trying to stop E.V.I.L.'s plans to destroy Grimm Academy, but Snow seems to be jinxing all their efforts. Her luck might change if she can find her own truly magical charm — before it falls into E.V.I.L. hands!

Rapunzel's enchanted, fast-growing hair can be a nuisance, especially when an accident gives it magical powers she can't control! But Rapunzel can't let her grimmorrible hair woes distract her — she and her friends Cinda, Red, and Snow are trying to save Grimm Academy from the E.V.I.L. Society. Once Rapunzel tracks down her magic charm, she won't let a bad hair day get in the way of stopping E.V.I.L.!

Sleeping Beauty — who just goes by her middle name, Rose — has always been a daredevil. But according to her fairy tale, after her twelfth birthday Rose must avoid all sharp objects. That isn't easy at Grimm Academy, where enchanted items can also be dangerous. Rose will have to stay wide awake to keep out of trouble — and to join the fight against E.V.I.L.!

Goldilocks is so eager to make friends at Grimm Academy, she's even tempted to accept an invitation to join E.V.I.L. — it's just nice to be included! But she doesn't want to be a villain. Can Goldie get inside the secret society and do some good?

Snowflake isn't sure which fairy-tale character she is. But with her magical powers causing lots of trouble, she's definitely on thin ice! So just in case she might be a villain, Snowflake is chilly to her classmates. Can she keep her cool until she knows her whole story, or will her social life at Grimm Academy be permanently *frozen*?

How to spot a 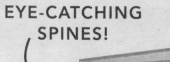 book

EYE-CATCHING
SPINES!

FUN &
FRIENDSHIP
INSIDE!

IRRESISTIBLE
STORIES!

PLUS,
FIRST
CRUSHES!